Unlocking the Mysteries of Rocket Science

Unlocking the Mysteries of Rocket Science

Dr. P. SASIKUMAR

Translated by

M. JOTHI MANI

**UNLOCKING THE MYSTERIES OF
ROCKET SCIENCE**
Dr. P. SASIKUMAR

Translated by **M. JOTHI MANI**

First Published: July, 2023

Published by

INDIAN UNIVERSITIES PRESS

Imprint of Bharathi Puthakalayam

7, Elango Salai, Teynampet, Chennai - 600 018

044 -24332424, 24332924, 24330024

Email: bharathiputhakalam@gmail.com | www.thamizhbooks.com

This book is a tribute to Dr. Vikram Sarabhai, who dreamed of India progressing in space technology and laid out an ideal path for its advancement

Foreword-I

Throw a half-full bottle of water over the top. When the bottle is in hand, the water is in the bottom most part. But surprisingly, in a thrown bottle, if the bottle decelerates, causing the inner water mass to move to the top and the water stays at the top of the bottle due to the upward force. Similarly, in an upward-rising launch vehicle, the liquid fuel flows into the upper part of the cylinder. How does that fuel flow towards the engine and burn in the combustion chamber to generate force?

Wouldn't that cause side-to-side rocking fuel forces that would also cause trouble in the launch vehicle's propulsion? How do launch vehicle engineers deal with this? While describing these questions, our curiosity to know the answer is stimulated, isn't it? This book raises various subtle questions and answers them in a way that stimulates our thinking.

If science is to reach the public, the content must be deep, and the way of speaking should also be attractive. It begins as usual like Galileo, adopting a narrative strategy in dissemination, especially in communicating science to the public through writing. From Mary Shelley, who played a major role in bringing science to the public in English, many others have used the narrative strategy.

However, this strategy is not easy to use effectively. Science should be told through the same creative elements as in a short story or novel. It's like walking on a knife. If not handled properly, there will be a lot of fictional incidents, and the science will become shallow, or the simplicity of one person asking a question and the other answering will be boring.

This book, written by my best friend of ISRO and a science writer, Dr. P. Sasikumar, is an excellent example of the narrative style. Some of the students who won the essay competition, accompanied by a scientist, visit the factory where the rocket is made. While going department-wise, they get to know the science embedded there.

Various models of rockets, carrying both crew and satellites, were on display. One student inquired why the weight of the rockets was measured in tons, while the weight of the satellites destined for space was in kilograms. The student approached a leading rocket expert for answers. The author beautifully explained the technical concept of payload ratio, comparing it to a bicycle carrying two individuals weighing a hundred kilograms combined, despite only weighing twenty kilograms itself. The combined weight of passengers and packages is only a fraction of a rocket's weight.

When reading about rocket technology, we inevitably have doubts and questions. The students in the story ask these questions, which the book brilliantly answers, explaining deep scientific ideas with ease.

Author Dr.P. Sasikumar wrote this book from his experience of explaining space technology to school and college students. He has a way of anticipating the questions that arise in our minds and answering them, akin to the Tamil proverb "palm like gooseberry."

While a truck has a fixed carrying capacity, the maximum weight a launch vehicle can carry depends on the destination in space. For example, the Falcon launch vehicle can place a 63-ton satellite in 1,000 kilometers above Earth, but only 23 tons of satellite in geostationary orbit, and 16 tons to Mars. This book provides an easy-to-understand answer to such technical questions, including why the first stage of a multi-stage aircraft typically uses solid fuel to produce more thrust during takeoff.

The author describes the history of missile technology, tracing it back to its origins in Mongolia and China, its development by Tippusultan of Mysore in India, and its use by the Nazis to attack England during World War II. This history also clarifies the differences between missiles and launch vehicles.

Information such as "We can use sugar and potassium nitrate to make rocket fuel" provides our body with energy. When pedaling a bicycle, we can generate a force of at most 25 to 30 percent of our body weight, while an elephant can generate about 7 tons of force. The book is full of fascinating information, such as "a rocket will produce 3500 tons of force, equal to a thousand elephants". Additionally, the book introduces us to modern technologies like cryogenics.

Furthermore, the author describes simple experiments that parents, teachers, and students can do at home or in school, such as launching an air-filled balloon or a toy with pressurized air-water. This is another highlight of the book.

I would like to express my appreciation to the Dr.P. Sasikumar, for this valuable book. I also request that the author may write about various fields of science in a simple and engaging manner, not only for parents, teachers, and students but also for those interested in learning how launch vehicles work. This book is a must-read for the general public seeking answers to questions about how ISRO launches spacecraft to Mars.

With love,
T.V. Venkateswaran,
Senior Scientist, Vigyan Prasar,
New Delhi.

Foreword-II

I am having close to twenty years of association with Dr. P. Sasikumar at official and personal level. I observed him as a young individual brimming with immense passion for all the activities he engaged in, be it composite product design/processing, statistical analysis, post-test analysis, or delivering lectures to school children. On every occasion, I witnessed him giving his utmost dedication. There was no doubt in our minds that he would go on to achieve remarkable success in his pursuits.

In the last few years, he has developed into a remarkable Tamil writer and has published books on a wide range of topics. These topics include astronauts, birds, trains, the universe, motivational concepts, day-to-day life science, and all of his works have been well-received by readers. One of his notable works is a book on rocket technology, which has been translated into English under the title "Unlocking the Mysteries of Rocket Science." This book provides a concise overview of the history of rockets and their working principles.

In this book, he presents the historical background and fundamental concepts of rocket science, including elementary design, experiments, and practical applications. The book delves into the core principles such as thrust, momentum, impulse, and the rocket equation. Furthermore, it explores the intricacies of rocket engines and their components. He also discusses different types of rocket engines, conducts a thorough examination of testing methods, and explores various subsystems involved in rocket technology.

The book introduces readers to topics such as payload and staging concepts, fundamental engine design (including liquid fuel, solid fuel, and hybrid fuel), systems engineering, integration, control systems, and a glimpse of system reusability. It also explains the differences between missiles and conventional rockets. This book is highly recommended as it covers almost all aspects of rocketry, which is sure to pique your interest in the subject. It is primarily aimed at beginners in rocket science or those who wish to expand their knowledge of the fundamentals of rocketry. The author presents the subject matter in a clear and concise manner, making it an excellent introduction even for non technical personnel.

The book's narrative style, presented in a question-and-answer format, further enhances the reader's engagement. The inclusion of do-it-yourself (DIY) experiments stimulates scientific curiosity and fosters a scientific mindset. In addition, it provides background information and explanations of scientific principles related to rocket flight. The book offers a variety of projects, experiments, and examples that are easily accessible and will captivate the attention of young minds. Written in straightforward English, the book also incorporates a few figures and tables for reference, aiding readers in visualizing concepts more effectively.

In summary, this book employs a writing style that can be understood by anyone, even those without technical knowledge. Personally, I found it thought-provoking, often prompting childhood questions in my mind. Clearly, the author possesses a deep passion for space and rockets, and has the ability to simplify complex ideas. With the increasing involvement of startups in rocket design and production, as well as the growing public interest in the field, this book will be in high demand as a valuable resource for understanding the basics of rocket science.

Mahesh V

Project Director, Solid motors group
VSSC/ISRO

Before We Start

It's worth noting that in casual conversation, the term "rocket science" is often used without a clear understanding of its meaning. Similarly, many people use the term "launch vehicle" without fully comprehending it. It's no exaggeration to say that students may find the science of launch vehicles daunting.

As part of the World Space Week celebrations, I had the opportunity to speak to college students in recent years. Additionally, I have spoken to secondary school students about rocket technology, and I have encountered more curiosity driven questions from students.

Every time I take classes, I self-examine my speech on how to explain difficult technology in an easy way, and I try to simplify it with materials and activities that school students experience in their daily lives.

In busy office schedule, It is not possible to visit all schools and speak with students individually. Therefore, the book has evolved to reach all students through its contents. I have created chapters focused on my classes on launch vehicles. The examples I have mentioned here are intended to simplify the speech.

I have practiced the methodology of explaining complex systems with the help of simple examples during my interactions with school children and the general public. This book is written in the same style as my class. Moreover, the examples quoted in this book have been well received by the audience.

A launch vehicle is utilized to transport an object from the surface of the Earth to a specific orbit around it. The intricate technology behind this process is extensively described in the book you are currently reading. To delve deeper into the workings of satellites in a fixed orbit and the various challenges faced by humans in space, I highly recommend exploring my book titled "Sky Riders."

I would like to express my gratitude to Atma Ravi, who has drawn the necessary images as beautiful pictures for the Tamil version of this book that perfectly matches my vision.

I express my heartfelt gratitude to my wife, Jothi Mani, and my son, Abhinav, for their dedicated efforts in translating this book from its original Tamil version into English.

I express my sincere gratitude to Dr. T. V. Venkateswaran, who carefully read Tamil version of this book and provided me with great insight amid his heavy workload.

I also extend my thanks to Karthikeyan and Prasanna who read the book and helped to improve the contents.

I would like to express my sincere gratitude to Shri V. Mahesh, the project director of the S200 solid motor at VSSC, ISRO. I am deeply thankful for his invaluable time and insightful technical suggestions, which greatly improved the clarity of this book. Furthermore, I am appreciative of his valuable input and perspectives shared for this publication.

Thiruvananthapuram,
18-06-2023

Dr. P. Sasikumar
writersasibooks@gmail.com

Story Field

An essay competition has been taken place to generate scientific interest in space science among students. Thousands of students from different parts of the country participated. An interview was being conducted for students who have specially formulated their imaginations in letters, and only the selected students had the opportunity to visit the launch vehicle manufacturing place.

Everything required for a launch vehicle is in one complex. Students from diverse cultural backgrounds participated in the competition. This book centers on the story of how each student navigates and understands the campus and rocket technology.

This book covers wider topics such as how a launch vehicle is made, how it carries materials to space, its capacity and monitoring, which is the world's largest launch vehicle, what are the challenges which exist in this technology, how they have overcome high temperatures, and how it differs from a missile etc.

During this fascinating conversation between students and scientists, you were just as amazed as the students were to learn about rockets. Best wishes from the author to all readers.

Contents

1
Rocket – An Introduction

Students from different parts of the country were waiting eagerly at the auditorium to learn about rocket technology. Each student introduced themselves and made friends by sharing information about their hometown and school. Then, the senior scientist of the space industry welcomed everyone and explained what they were going to learn the next few days. The first lesson started with an explanation of the principles of rockets. The students were advised that they could ask any doubts they had during the session.

Why a modern man requires rockets?

Empires began to form during the dawn of human civilization. The emperors of these empires wanted to expand their kingdoms. It became customary to wage war on neighboring countries to extend their territories. Each nation used its military powers to bring the enemy's soldiers to their knees and usurp their throne.

During times of war, there arose a necessity for weapons capable of traversing vast distances to engage the enemy from afar. Consequently, rockets were devised with this specific intent. These projectiles were initially employed in the 13th-century AD conflict between the Chinese and the Mongols; however, their range was rather limited at that time. Subsequently, with the advent of gunpowder, the rockets' efficacy escalated significantly, leading to their expanded utilization.

Tippusultan is said to be the first emperor in the world to have successfully used missiles in his army. He repulsed the British with his missiles in the battles at Mysore at the end of the eighteenth century. Later, Tippusultan's missiles were confiscated by the British, and the technology was explored and new missiles were developed. This helped the British forces to conquer other parts of India easily.

140 years later, during World War II, the development of modern missiles was initiated by Germany under the leadership of Hitler. The V-2 missiles he developed proved highly effective in attacking enemy nations. Hitler oversaw the production of over six thousand missiles, deploying more than three thousand of them against enemy countries. Following Hitler's demise, missile technology underwent further advancements by the United States and Russia, leading to significant progress in this field.

When you said "first" you mentioned missiles. However, we typically refer to the vehicle that carries humans into space as a launch vehicle. What is the reason for these different names?

The vehicle that goes from the ground to the sky is typically called a rocket, and its name changes depending on its purpose. When a rocket takes off from one location on Earth and carries weapons of destruction, like bomb, to another location, it is called a missile. So, in a way, launch vehicle can be seen as vessel for construction, while missile, a carrier for destruction.

Missiles are often used by countries' armies to demonstrate their military power. A country's military strength can be determined by the distance and range of their missiles. For instance, Russia's RS-28 is a long-range intercontinental ballistic missile that can travel up to 18,000 kilometers which equals to half circumference of the earth.

On the other hand, we refer to rocket as a launch vehicle when it is used to transport payloads from Earth to space. This may include satellites / spacecraft, construction materials for building a space station, food for the astronauts in the space station, or a space ships for carrying humans.

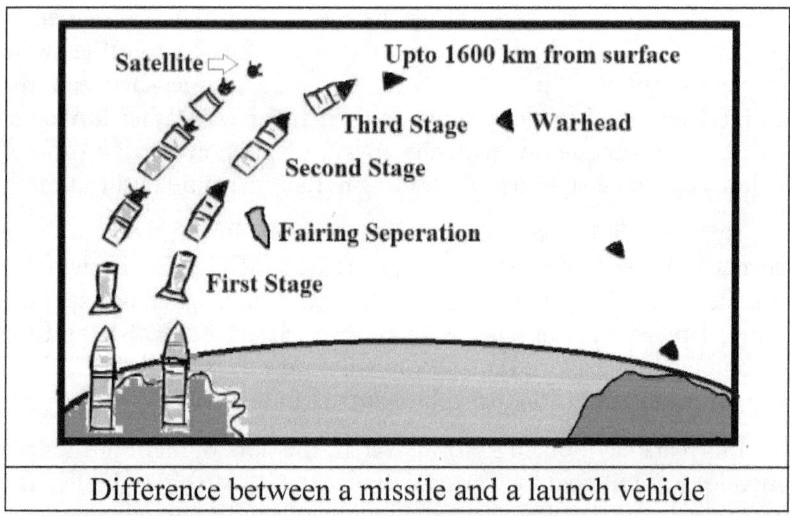

Difference between a missile and a launch vehicle

Whether attacking the enemy country is ok? Why do we need to take objects into space, and what are the benefits for us?

Throughout the past century, we have designed and developed numerous devices that have significantly improved our lives. It is no exaggeration to say that they have changed our lives beyond imagination. One such application is using objects in the sky to perform tasks that we need.

We can only communicate with someone if they can hear or see us. When it comes to observing large areas, such as countries on Earth, we can achieve this by gaining higher elevation. Similar to how we can sit atop a mountain and overlook numerous villages or cities, we can view multiple countries by ascending into the sky.

For instance, how can we watch football and cricket matches conducted from other countries live in our homes? Satellites orbiting in the sky perform this task effectively. They play a crucial role in transmitting messages from the football field to the sky within seconds and broadcasting them to all countries.

They also analyze wind and clouds pattern, informing us of upcoming storms and rainfall patterns. It is easier to predict crop growth, disease outbreaks, and the likelihood of dam breaches when viewed from above.

We send satellites into space to perform such tasks meticulously. Launch vehicles are essential in positioning these satellites at a specific orbit above the Earth's surface. Similarly, these launch vehicles support human transportation to space stations, where they conduct research and experiments/explorations.

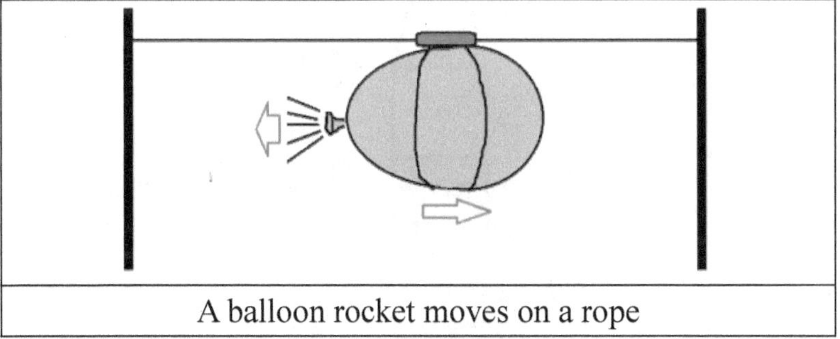

A balloon rocket moves on a rope

Doesn't Newton's theory explain how rocket lifted? If so, what distinguishes rockets from ordinary vehicles we see on the ground?

Rocket goes upwards as per the Newton's Third law "For every action there is an equal and opposite reaction". The launch vehicle needs many times more thrust than the vehicle we see on the ground such as buses on the roads, and trains on the railway tracks. Rolling a ball on floor is easy, but try throwing it up.

We will learn in the coming days why the launch vehicle needs to travel at several times the speed of ground vehicles and also travels against the force of gravity to launch the satellite in a certain orbit. It will be covered.

Today's theoretical concepts of rocket class has ended, and practical classes on how the rocket works will begin. Everyone eagerly rushed to the ground to prepare the working model of flying rocket and was trained to design water and wind-powered rockets.

Each person was given a balloon to experiment with. When the balloon is filled with air and released, the high-pressure air inside tries to escape, creating a force that pushes the balloon in the opposite direction. Depending on how they held the balloon, it flew in different directions.

A thread was tied between two trees to keep the air coming out of the balloon in a uniform direction. A small straw was introduced to the thread that could be moved with low friction. An air-filled balloon was bonded to the straw. When the balloon mouth was opened, the air from the balloon rushed out, the balloon continued its journey from one direction to another by sliding through the thread.

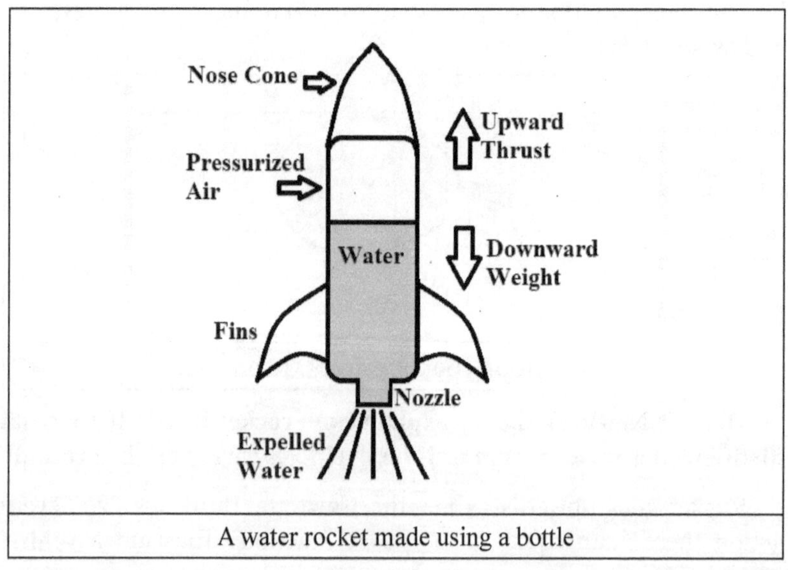

A water rocket made using a bottle

The class was also excited to learn about making air-blown water bottles. The pressure inside the water bottle was increased with a bicycle pump, and the pressure was released when it reached three to four times atmospheric pressure. The high-pressure air inside the bottle tried to escape through the hole, creating a driving force that made the bottle fly upwards.

Next, they made a water launch vehicle by filling the bottle with water and slowly increasing the pressure by injecting air. Since water is the pressuring medium the bottle pressure can be higher compare to air bottle. When the bottle was released, the water gushed out through the small opening, resulting in the movement of bottle upwards.

They explained that the gases are ejected under high velocity, and the higher the pressure and temperature of the gas being burned, the greater the upward force from it. The launch vehicle's engines are designed to store sufficient quantity of required fuels for few minutes of operations of the rocket.

As everyone dispersed with interest to learn more in the coming classes, one student chanted that the human body is powered by air and the air filled in the bus tire helps to carry passengers. Ultimately the hot air released via nozzles creates the thrust required to propel the rockets upwards.

2
Which objects should go to space?

Although the students had studied the principles of rocket in many textbooks, they were thrilled to see flying bottles and moving balloons when conducting rocket launch experiments for the first time, allowing them to grasp the concept of rocket launching. In their next class, they attended a session on "What should be taken to space?"

The students saw various satellites that had gone into space and models of spaceships that could carry humans. Satellites are equipped with antennas and transponders to receive signals from earth station. The transmitting antennas in satellite are used to transmit them back to other parts of the earth. Additionally, there was a set of solar panels to generate necessary electricity from sunlight. A model of the launch vehicle that would carry the satellite into space was also displayed next to it.

The launch vehicle displayed here is very large and tall. You have specified its weight in tons, but the weight of the satellites and spaceships which carried by launch vehicle is only given in kilograms. Based on this observation, a student asked, "Why couldn't we carry a larger object?"

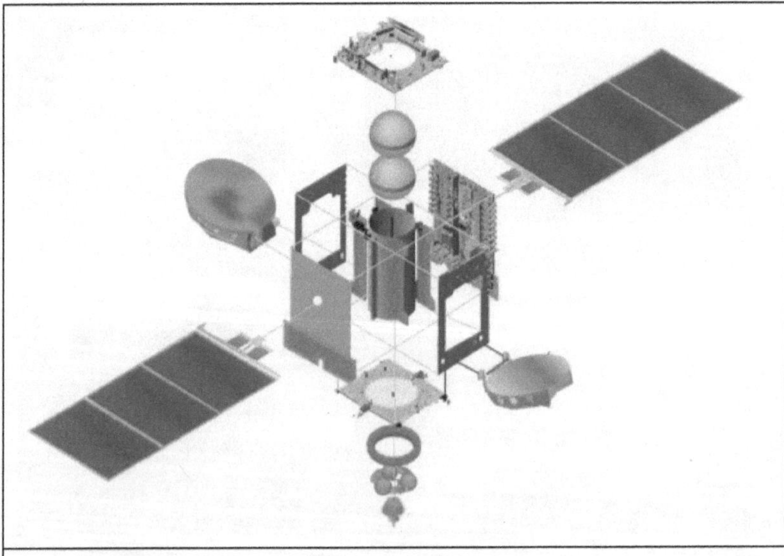

Typical parts of a satellite. Solar panels to generate electricity, antenna and reflector to communicate with Earth, fuel tanks, small thrusters for controlling etc.

Before delving into the payload of the launch vehicle, let us first understand the carrying capacity of transport vehicles around us. The scientist who was explaining about this question asked a boy in the first row, "Do you know how to ride a bicycle?" he inquired.

The boy excitedly replied, "I go to school by bicycle only." The scientist then asked, "Can you take your friend along with you on a bicycle ride?" The boy replied, "Definitely possible, we have traveled many times like that." This means a bicycle weighing around 20 kg is capable of carrying both of them. Assuming both of them weigh 100 kg, the bicycle can carry five times its weight.

The scientist then asked if anyone knew about a two-wheeler like a bicycle. A girl sitting on the last bench said, "Recently, my mom bought a new bike. I saw that the weight of the vehicle was written as 130 kg. I, my younger brother, and my mother can travel in it. The sum of the weight of the three of us would be equal to the weight of our new two-wheeler."

Here, the two-wheeler has the capacity to carry a weight equal to its own weight. If we consider a 1000 Kg car, it can carry thirty to forty percent of its weight as goods and people that is equal to 300 to 400 Kg.

In contrast, airplanes that are flying weigh in several tons. The world's heaviest plane weighs 600 tons when all passengers are loaded. The weight of material it can lift is only one-fourth of its total weight. We have observed that the aforementioned vehicles have reduced their weight-carrying capacity from five times to just 25 percent of empty weight.

If we compare this with the weight of a launch vehicle, a launch vehicle can carry only 1% to 4% of its weight, and this varies depending on how far and at what speed, we have to inject the satellite or spaceships into space.

Oh, really! Can a launch vehicle with such a heavy weight carry the least amount of weight to space? Why can't it carry more things like a bicycle?

In the vehicles mentioned earlier, a bicycle has a speed of 10-20 kmph, while a car travels at a speed of 100 kmph. Similarly, an airplane travels at a speed of 600-900 kilometers per hour. However, to orbit the objects in space, we need to achieve an extremely high velocity, which is much greater than any of these vehicles.

Energy is required to move anything. For us to walk, run, jump etc. But we can easily realize that walking or running is more energy efficient to move from one place to other than Jumping or hopping like a frog. This is because, while we do work against gravity during jumping, we nearly move perpendicular to gravity, while walking or running, requiring lesser energy. Just like in jumping, launch vehicles also need to work against gravity and hence needs more energy, which is packed in the propulsion system, making them very heavy vehicle, for given mass.

The reason why a launch vehicle cannot carry more weight is that, to orbit objects in space, they must be launched at a velocity of 20,000 to 30,000 kilometers per hour and also travelling against gravity unlike ground vehicle and airplanes. Achieving such high speed requires a lot of fuel, which increases the weight of the launch vehicle.

Therefore, a launch vehicle must carry a significant amount of fuel to work against gravity and attain the necessary velocity to put the object into space. This results in a trade-off between the weight of the payload and the amount of fuel required to achieve the necessary velocity.

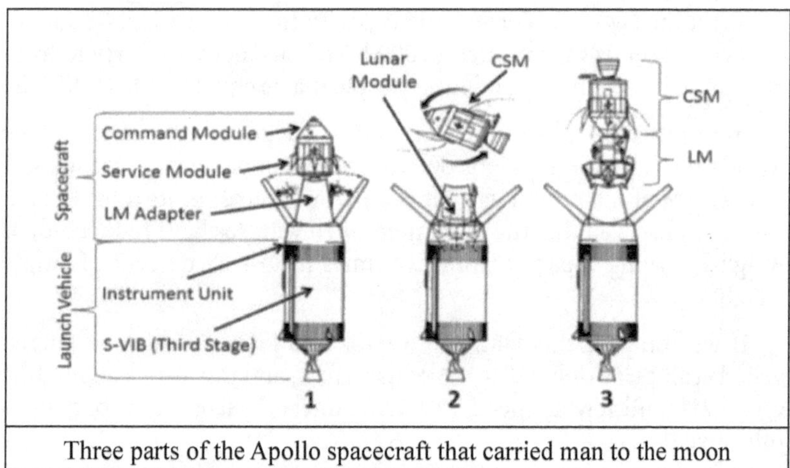

Three parts of the Apollo spacecraft that carried man to the moon

"Does it require more energy to get beyond the air to the outer atmosphere?"

Yes, it does require more energy to get beyond the air to the outer atmosphere. When a launch vehicle ascends through the atmosphere, it experiences resistance from the air, which is known as drag. All vehicles on the ground require fuel to run, but oxygen is necessary for any substance to burn, which is obtained from the atmospheric air when we are in the atmosphere.

For instance, the petrol used in our vehicles requires 14.5 times its weight of air to burn, and firewood requires 5 to 8 kg of air to burn per kg of wood. Oxygen is the densest of gases, therefore oxygen is more abundant in the surface of earth atmosphere compared to other gases and decreases with altitude.

When atmospheric air has less than 16 percent oxygen, it is difficult to burn things. This is why wood cannot be burned in the normal atmosphere in mountainous regions above 15 thousand feet.

Soyuz spacecraft of the Soviet Union, which had sent humans into space more than a hundred times

A launch vehicle cannot get oxygen like a ground vehicle, since we would have to travel in space which is vacuum. Hence, oxygen must be carried along with the required fuel, which adds to the total weight. This is also the main reason why the weight of the launch vehicle increases.

Since a bicycle does not require any fuel to function, as it is manually propelled, it can be assumed that it has no fuel. When the fuel tank of a two-wheeler is fully filled, it will have a weight of 5 to 10 percent of the total weight of the vehicle. For a car, it is a little more than 5 percent. Due to the high speed and long non-stop travel, the amount of fuel that an airplane takes can be up to 25 percent of its total weight.

But in all these types of transportation vehicles, we must understand that the oxygen required to burn the fuel is taken only from the air. If these vehicles were forced to carry the necessary air, the amount of fuel and air required by them would be more than the weight of the vehicle.

Like a launch vehicle, if a car and an airplane carry their own oxygen. They can carry materials only 15-20 percent of their own weight. Similarly, an airplane can carry goods and people less than 10 percent of its own weight.

We know that water contains oxygen just as air does. That is why fish live by breathing oxygen in water. Are there other types of oxygen? That's fascinating.

We cannot directly store pure solid oxygen in a cylinder and run the engine of a launch vehicle. Instead, oxygen must be obtained from solid and liquid materials, which we call oxidizer. When we transport solid and liquid materials that can produce oxygen, only some percent of oxidizer is converted to useful oxygen. This oxygen product weighs two to three times as much as fuel. So if you add the fuel and the oxygen-generating material needed to burn it, it will be more than 80 percent of the total weight of the launch vehicle.

"Want to carry so many things?" wondered a student.

"Yes, firstly the fuel, secondly the substances that can generate the oxygen required for the fuel to burn. And because of their higher weight, they should be kept in a container, which will be explained to you in the upcoming classes," replied the scientist.

Another student was looking at a launch vehicle whose weight was written as 500 tons and wondered if a thousand students from his school would equal this weight. He began to calculate.

Then his friend who came there showed him his calculation that the weight of 500 tons is obtained by adding the total weight of the students in 10 schools where a thousand students study, just like their school.

Similarly, scaled model of launch vehicle were kept. The actual height of the launch vehicle mentioned as 50 meters. Another girl wondered if all 30 of them in the class could reach the height of the launch vehicle if they stood one on the other. The scientist said that in the next class they would learn how to make a high-powered launch vehicle, not only large ones but also many smaller ones.

3
Energy of the launch vehicle

As students were amazed by the size of the launch vehicle, they entered the next building while wondering to themselves, "How can the launch vehicle carry such a huge weight?"

"Sir, we saw in the last class that a launch vehicle can weigh several tons. Don't we need a more powerful engine to transport such a heavy object?" one student asked.

"Rightly said," the scientist replied. "As the launch vehicle takes off from the launch pad, the upward thrust must be at least 20 percent greater than its weight. For example, a launch vehicle weighing 500 tons must have more than 600 tons of upward thrust when it takes off."

A girl asked her friend, "How many elephants weigh 600 tons?" The scientist observed the student and replied, "Normally, the pulling and pushing forces of animals depend on their body structure. Our bodies have skeletal and muscular systems, and pushing beyond a certain force can damage our body parts. The human body can generate a maximum of 25 to 30 percent of its body weight. Attempting to generate more force than this can result in bone fractures and muscle tears Weightlifters need special training to strengthen their legs and arms, to lift heavy weights. Now, let's address your question. Indian elephants typically weigh an average of 3 tons, while African elephants can reach weights of up to 5 tons. I hope this provides you with the answer you were seeking.".

Think of our journey on a bicycle. We apply force to the bicycle pedaling with our feet, which propels the bicycle forward. The speed of the bicycle slows down when traveling on a steep road compared to a flat surface. If the force from our feet is not enough to propel the bicycle, it will stop. When we apply too much force, we may experience problems such as knee pain or broken bones.

Similarly, an elephant can generate a force of up to 7 tons. However, it is understood that more energy is required to propel a rocket upward. The question is whether it is possible to generate enough energy from a single engine to achieve this.

It is understood that more energy is required to propel the rocket upward. "Is it possible to generate enough energy to propel the rocket through single engine?

Saturn-V can generate 3500 tons of thrust, equivalent to a thousand elephants. The first stage of the rocket and its creator, Wernher von Braun.

A small launch vehicle may have a single engine to provide the necessary power. However, if there isn't an engine that can generate enough thrust, we can combine multiple small engines to achieve the required thrust. This can be compared to the horse-drawn carts of the olden days, where several horses were hitched to a single carriage to pull a heavy load. In the upcoming classes, you will learn about how these engines are attached to the launch vehicle.

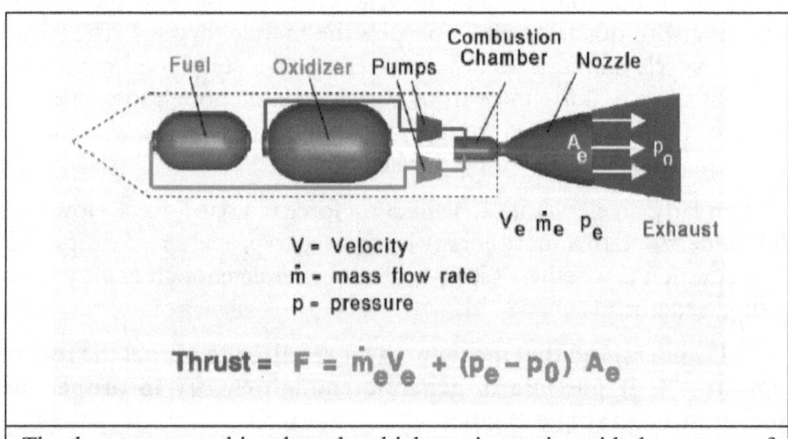

The thrust generated in a launch vehicle engine varies with the amount of gases coming from its nozzle and its velocity

It is understood that the launch vehicle acquires force according to Newton's third law. But can you explain clearly how the combustion gases in a cylinder are converted into force?

In the previous classes you have attended, you might have noticed that the air escapes from the balloon through a small hole. To find out how much force the air creates, we get the answer by multiplying quantity of expelled air each second and how fast the air came out.

If we increase the mass flow rate or velocity of the burnt gases coming out of the nozzle, we can generate more thrust. When we perform this process within Earth's atmosphere, the pressure of the air coming out of the nozzle is equivalent to atmospheric pressure. However, the vehicle gradually takes off from one atmospheric pressure and proceeds into an airless vacuum. This creates an additional thrust for the launch vehicle as there is a difference between the exhaust pressure coming out of the nozzle and the atmospheric pressure.

"It is understood that when more fuel can be burnt the mass flow rate of exhaust gas is increased. But how can their exit velocity be increased?

The combustion of the gases in the rocket engine takes place at a specific temperature and pressure. This pressure and heat are converted into kinetic energy, and the burnt gases are expelled at high velocity. By increasing the temperature and pressure of the combustibles, the velocity of the exhaust gases can be increased. Just like we bring our mouth in a specific shape, to create whistle sound, by increasing the air velocity, rockets use nozzle, to shape the exhaust flow and increase it velocity.

The air that fills our bicycle tires is typically at a pressure of two to three bar. In a bus, five to six bar of pressure is sufficient to carry 50 passengers. Normally, the pressure in the combustion zone of a launch vehicle is 40 to 60 bar. Liquid engines operating at a pressure of 300 bar are also in use.

What is the types of fuel used in the launch vehicle?

The launch vehicle uses either solid or liquid or combination of solid and liquid. You will learn about them clearly in upcoming classes.

Does the pressure generated in a launch vehicle engine remain constant, or does it vary as the vehicle moves?

When the air comes out of a balloon, the pressure is initially high, causing air to exit at a high velocity. As the air pressure decreases, so does the velocity of the expelled air. However, since the rocket engine continuously burns fuel, the pressure can be kept constant.

In the case of liquid fuels, the amount of combustible material can be accurately measured and injected into the combustion chamber. Therefore, in liquid engines, the pressure remains constant during combustion. However, in solid fuel, they are stored in a cylindrical motor case and burn from the center to outward. The pressure varies depending on how much of the fuel burns at a given instant.

Is it true that both solid and liquid fuels produce the same amount of force?

Generally, more thrust can be generated by rockets that are typically powered by solid fuel. There were solid rockets capable of generating 1800 tons of force. At the same time, it is difficult to develop liquid engines that can generate high force. In Raptor liquid engine, 180 tons of force is generated. To achieve this the engine is operating at a pressure of 300 bar. The liquid engine used in the Saturn-V launch vehicle that carried humans to the moon was designed to produce 700 tons of thrust, even though it was operated at a lower pressure. It is important to understand that the efficiency of an engine running at high pressure is greater than an engine running at low pressure.

If so, do solid engines take advantage over liquid engines during lift off because they produce more thrust? A student raised the question.

You are correct. Solid propellant engines are generally preferred for their ability to generate high thrust, which is necessary during launch vehicle lift off. However, small liquid engines can also be used in cluster to generate the sufficient lift off thrust. For example, NASA's Space Shuttle launch vehicle had two solid motor straurons that helped lift the launch vehicle from the ground. Each solid motor was generating a thrust of 1,200 tons.

Similarly, Space-X's Falcon-heavy launch vehicle is fully powered by liquid engines, with two liquid-fueled strapons engines used to propel it from the launch pad. Each of these engines is connected to nine smaller liquid engines, which together can generate a force of 770 tons. The 1400-ton launch vehicle takes off from Earth using these liquid engine strapons. The Saturn-V launch vehicle, which carried humans to the moon, was also powered entirely by a liquid engine. The 3000 ton Saturn-V lifted from ground using five liquid engines each one capable of producing 700 tons of thrust.

"You mentioned that the weight carried by the launch vehicle changes based on the distance it needs to travel in space, but it's not clear by how much it varies."

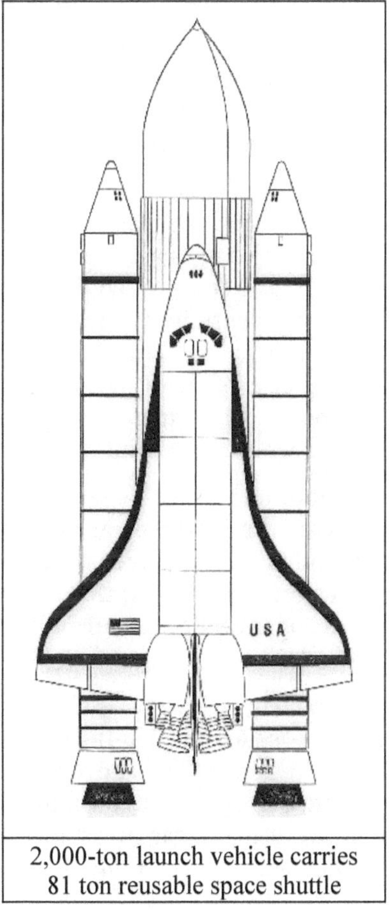

2,000-ton launch vehicle carries
81 ton reusable space shuttle

If the aforementioned heavy Falcon launch vehicle continues its 1,400-ton journey, it will be able to deploy a 63-ton payload at low earth orbit (LEO) (400 to 1,000 kilometers orbit). However, if it needs to be placed at height of 36,000 kilometers from Earth, it can carry only 26 tons of weight.

Let's not consider Earth anymore. If the launch vehicle wants to break out of Earth's gravity and land on Mars, it can safely deliver 16 tons of material to Mars. If it needs to go even further, this rocket can carry 3 tons of material to Pluto. In the following classes, you will learn about the potential energy and kinetic energy needed to propel an object into space.

When my father last time bought a car, he searched for one that would provide the best mileage per liter of petrol. Additionally, among the many rocket motors and engines you mentioned, which one is the best? How can we determine that? Which parameters dictates the same?

To determine the efficiency of a launch vehicle, specific impulse (Isp) is considered. This measures the duration of thrust that can be generated when one kilogram of fuel is taken and one kilogram of thrust is generated.

The specific impulse of each propellant indicates its efficiency. For example, engines that use solid fuels are capable of providing specific thrust in the range of 220-260 seconds, while engines that use liquid fuels can provide specific thrust in the range of 300-320 seconds. Cryogenic fuels can operate at low temperatures (-150°C to -273°C) and have a specific impulse of over 400 seconds. Semi cryogenic engines are easy to store fuels compare to cryogenic fuel but their specific impulse at the order of 350 seconds.

A student asked about a message he learned in his school: "My science teacher said that the food we eat is converted into sugar, which is used for the body's energy needs, and that sugar is a fuel because it contains carbon. He also said that a launch vehicle can be made using powdered sugar and potassium nitrate. Could it really be a better launch vehicle?"

Your teacher is absolutely right. Potassium nitrate is the oxidant that provides the oxygen needed to burn the carbon and hydrogen in the sugar, which is the fuel. When these two are mixed, enough oxygen is obtained from the potassium nitrate to burn the carbon in the sugar. As this mixture is made using sugar, we sometimes call it 'Rocket Candy', just like the chocolates we eat. Only that 'Rocket candy' is for rockets to eat and not for us !!

For the complete combustion of sugar, it requires twice a weight of potassium nitrate to generate sufficient oxygen. This mixture packed in a wooden rod, they will go farther than your air and water bottle rockets. This type of fuel made from sugar has a lower specific impulse compared to the aforementioned solid and liquid fuel, ranging from 120 to 130 seconds.

"How would a 500-ton launch vehicle compare to the transport vehicles we see?"

Launching a vehicle of that weight would require the power of ten to fifteen trains, or the power of 200 trucks, or the power of 400 buses, or the power of one hundred thousand horses.

In the following classes, you will see clearly the types of fuels used in rocket engines. The manager who led the students announced that the class is over and they can go for lunch.

Two students were discussing as follows:

Is it already lunch time?

Time flies by, seemingly slipping through our fingers. We are unable to grasp even a single moment. The space industry has forged ahead, erecting colossal machines that stand as the pinnacle of human engineering. As they meander towards the canteen, their conversation revolves around the insurmountable dominance of the space department, leaving no room for competition

4
Solid Fuels

The students who had many doubts after the last class were surprised to learn that today's most popular launch vehicles obtain their kinetic energy from chemical energy. In chemical energy, the fuel undergoes a chemical reaction with oxygen to form gases. The kinetic energy is then obtained as these burnt gases exit through a nozzle attached to the tip of the rocket engine or motor at a high velocity. But then, this is also the way we humans are able to move, by converting the chemical energy in food we eat, to muscle movement, which is mechanical energy form.

The solid fuel operated rockets are called motor. Similarly, liquid fuel operated rockets are called engine.

They learned that fuels can exist in solid and liquid states, and that in this class they will be learning about how solid fuels are formed. As they entered the building with "Solid Fuel Manufacturing Area" written in big letters, they saw huge trucks parked outside and a large cylindrical drum.

"I can't imagine how they mix fuel and oxygen in solid fuel," said one of the students.

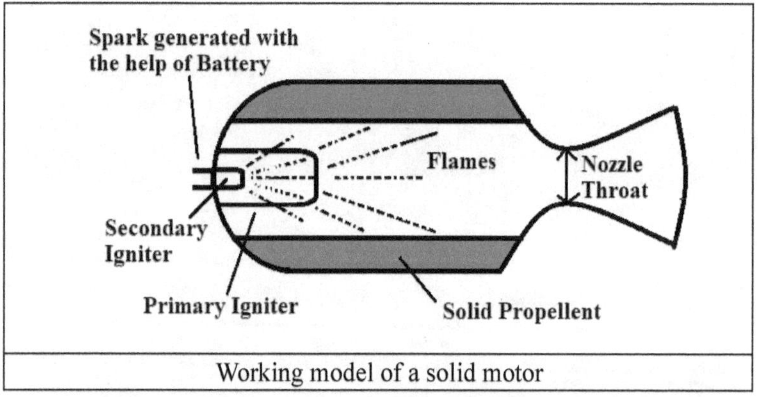

Working model of a solid motor

As mentioned earlier, fuel requires oxygen to burn. Even if we take the air in the atmosphere, it only contains 21% oxygen. Similarly, even if solid-state oxidizers are used, only a limited amount of oxygen will be available in them.

Since the weight of the launch vehicle should be low, lightweight elements such as aluminum and beryllium are used as fuel. These are taken as pulverized particles, up to 20% of the total weight. It also requires oxidizer such as ammonium perchlorate. Generally, the weight percentage of oxidizer is 3 to 4 times of solid fuel.

This fuel and oxidizer must be mixed together. Only when these two are present in the correct ratio in the mixture, the fuel will receive the oxygen it needs during combustion. Therefore, there is a need for an adhesive that can hold these two together.

About 10% bonding material such as HTPB or PBAN is also thoroughly mixed to form proper bond between fuel and oxidizer and to have required mechanical properties. The primary function of bonding materials is to hold fuel and oxygen together, but it also serves as a fuel source due to its carbon and hydrogen content. This is similar to Laddu, where Ghee is the binder that holder the sugar, cashews and flour together. Here, Ghee not only acts as a binder but also adds richness and flavor to the sweet.

It was surprising to see how finely the fuel and oxygen were pulverized in the reactor.

A girl asked, "You mentioned that these two materials should be powdered. When I grind rice flour for home use, I use different grain size for making puttu recipe and dosa. Is there a specific powder grain size that should be used for this process?"

This is a crucial question to consider. If you ask us to fill this glass jar with stones, it will fill quickly because the stones are larger. We can then fill the remainder of the jar with soil. If the soil is more powdery, we can continue to add more to the jar.

As particle size decreases, excess mass can be packed into a specific volume, by filling all available gaps or voids. The amount of excess that needs to be replenished depends on the fuel and oxidizer material. If we want the fuel to burn more quickly, we need to increase its surface area.

When a stone is broken into smaller pieces, the sum of the surface area of all the broken pieces is greater than the surface area of the original stone. Therefore, the grain size of solid fuel ingredients are a crucial factors to meet the requirements.

If it is to be in powder form, then how much size do we need, and why is it necessary?

These powders range in size from 50 to 300 microns, with the average size of a human hair being around 60 microns. Once solid fuel is ignited, it will continue to burn, and we use several methods to determine how much should be burned per second.

One method involves selecting fine particles, which increases its surface area and burning rate. Using a catalyst is another way to increase the rate at which solid fuel burns. There are many more methods like these, and solid propellants have been designed to burn at rates ranging from 3 to 20 millimeters per second.

Do we understand the need to change the rate of solid fuel burning?

The rate at which the fuel burns depends on the chemical reaction that results in the formation of gases. The chemical reaction takes place depending on the rate at which the fuel burns, which results in the formation of gases. If the burning speed is high, more gases are formed. When they exit through the nozzle, we get more thrust. Instant acceleration requires fuel that burns quickly after ignition.

If going slowly is enough, slow-burning fuel is sufficient. If something goes awry while the astronauts are traveling on the launch vehicle, the spaceship or crew module they are traveling will be separated from the launch vehicle and carry them to safety. Such modules requires high-thrust fuels to carry the astronauts and separate at higher speeds than the launch vehicle.

Everyone watched as the mixture was poured into a large cylindrical vessel. There was a mold in the middle, like a mold used to make jaggery balls from sugar, and the fuel mixture was poured around the mold. A small portion of the fuel poured into the big motor case was then poured into a small vessel also.

When asked what it was, they said, "We will find out the quality of the fuel made here by burning the little motor," as per the proverb "One grain suffices to test a whole pot of cooked rice."

How is a solid rocket prepared?

After mixing the necessary ingredients, they are kept in oven like idlis are made at home. To do this, the mixture is placed in a large oven and kept at a temperature of 60°C for about two to three days.

Once the fuel is ready, the mold placed in the middle is slowly removed. Everyone was surprised to see that the fuel inside each cylinder had a different shape, like circular, star-shaped, and lobe-shaped. They asked why this was the case and didn't understand the reason behind the various shapes.

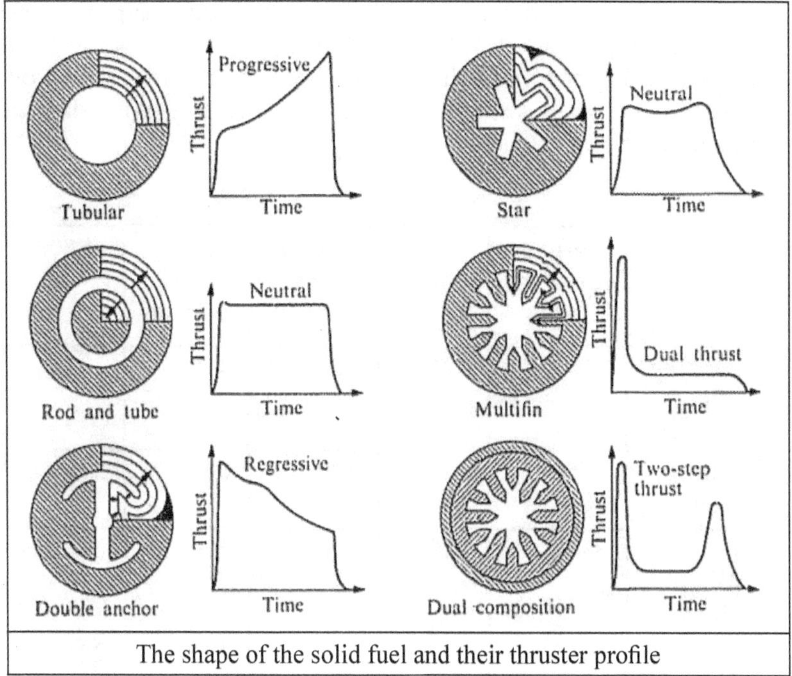

The shape of the solid fuel and their thruster profile

If we decide on the desired pressure for a liquid engine, we can maintain that pressure by injecting enough fuel into the combustion chamber. However, with solid fuel, the pressure varies from the beginning to the end of the burn. The fuel geometry design in the cylinder is determined by the pressure requirements.

Typically, the propellant used to lift the launch vehicle off the ground generates a lot of force at first to accomplish this. After a certain distance, the air's frictional force on the launch vehicle becomes too high, so the vehicle is designed to move more slowly, since going faster requires more energy. Once the vehicle has covered a certain distance, the fuel burning rate is adjusted to produce more force, which allows it to accelerate again. The various designs seen in rockets help to create this effect.

For the solid motors that operate in a vacuum, the fuel is loaded into a circular shape inside the cylinder, allowing more fuel to be loaded. In these motors, the generated force will continue to increase from the beginning to the end of the burn.

Solid fuel can be designed to be either regressive or progressive type, depending on how it is burned. As the temperature of the burnt materials during burning is more than 3000C, a thermal insulation, also known as rocket casing insulation, is created to prevent damage to the motor case.

Solid Motor	Saturn-booster 260in	SLS-SRM	Shuttle –SRM	P238 of Ariane	S200 of LVM3
Operating Time (seconds)	114	126	127	130	128
Thrust (Tons)	1750	1490	1200	665	515
Gross Weight (Tons)	831	730	590	270	236
Period of use	1965-67	2015-	1980-2011	1994-	2010-

"To produce a large thrust for several seconds, solid motor of larger length would be required. However, it is impossible to produce it in one piece, so it is divided into segments that are joined together after propellant casting. When segments are joined together axial burning of propellant should not be taken place at the joints. To ensure that inhibitor layers provided on either sides of the joining segments.

The Hitler's V2-Missile used liquid fuel engines and those days solid fuels were not widely used. If a liquid-fueled missile is to be launched, fuel is to be filled first, which can take few minutes. This means that missiles cannot be launched immediately. Moreover, during the fuel filling process, there is a high chance of an accident, which could cause damage to the entire launch system if it was hit by enemy missiles or bombs. High-speed fueling systems and tunnel refueling systems were designed for this purpose."

 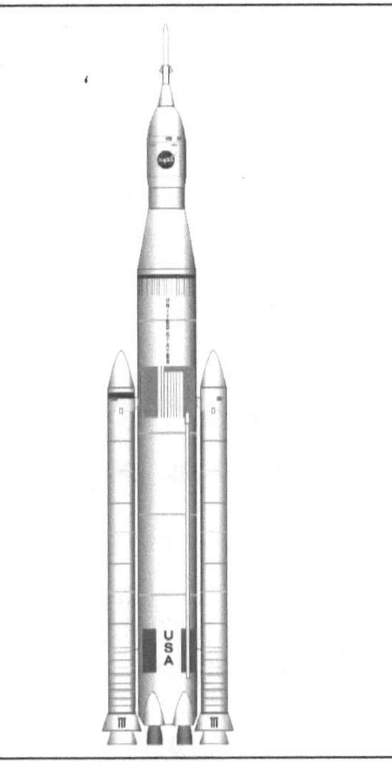

Ariane 5 launch vehicle. The 2 sold motor strapons are capable of generating 665 tons of thrust	2 solid motor strapons of NASA's SLS vehicle capable of generating 1490 tons of thrust

"As solid propellants progressed, they played an increasingly important role in missile technology. This was mainly due to the fact that solid-fueled missiles ready to launch than liquid-fueled missiles, as they were not needed last minutes operations like fueling.

Does the efficiency of a solid fuel engine decrease if it is left unused for several days? Is there an expiry date?

Solid fuels stored properly can last for many years. However, due to the self-weight of the propellant and seasonal temperature variations, there is a possibility of slight variations in performance and minor loss in efficiency. These issues can be minimized by adopting appropriate storage methods.

Two girls mentioned that typically, solid fuels contain about 70 percent of oxidizer. This composition provides the necessary oxygen for combustion. Additionally, we can appreciate that our buses and two-wheelers use oxygen from the atmosphere, rather than having to carry oxygen with them. This is a testament to the generosity of Mother Earth.

5
Liquid fuels

All the students arrived at the liquid engine manufacturing facility, and their surprise subsided as they observed how solid propellants are filled into containers several meters in height and diameter. They noticed many little pipes floating around, and the manager of the liquid fuel facility began explaining to them about the liquid fuel engine. They resembled the pipes to the nervous system in the human body.

The liquid rocket engine was born when Robert Hutchings Goddard (1882–1945) launched a rocket powered by a liquid fuel that functioned through petrol and liquid oxygen in 1926. This period saw the invention of many types of machines, including those powered by petrol and diesel, as well as the demonstration of flying airplanes.

An engine that could run on petrol helped the Wright brothers to fly, and similarly, Goddard's first experiment with the liquid fuel engine was successful due to his research into straight flight. The liquid fuel engine flew for only 2.5 seconds, rising up to a height of 12 meters before falling 50 meters away from the launching site.

Liquid fuel played an important role in the first missiles and launch vehicle engines ever invented. Hitler's V-2 rocket, the world's first long-range missile, used liquid ethanol as fuel along with liquid oxygen.

Liquid fuel was used in all three stages of the Saturn-V launch vehicle that carried humans into Moon.

While you mentioned that the Chinese were the first to develop rockets, it's also worth noting that Tippusultan developed missiles using solid propellant as we learnt. So how did liquid fuel engines take over as the preferred choice in first generation rockets?

Although the launch vehicles built by the Chinese and the missiles built by Tippusultan were made of solid materials, the gunpowder used in them was not very effective Just like steam locomotive using coal. Solid fuel research gained importance only after World War II. The solid rocket played an important role in the launch vehicle that carried the US space shuttle. All previous launch vehicles used liquid propellants.

As he explained the history of rocket engine fuels, he began to talk about liquid propellants.

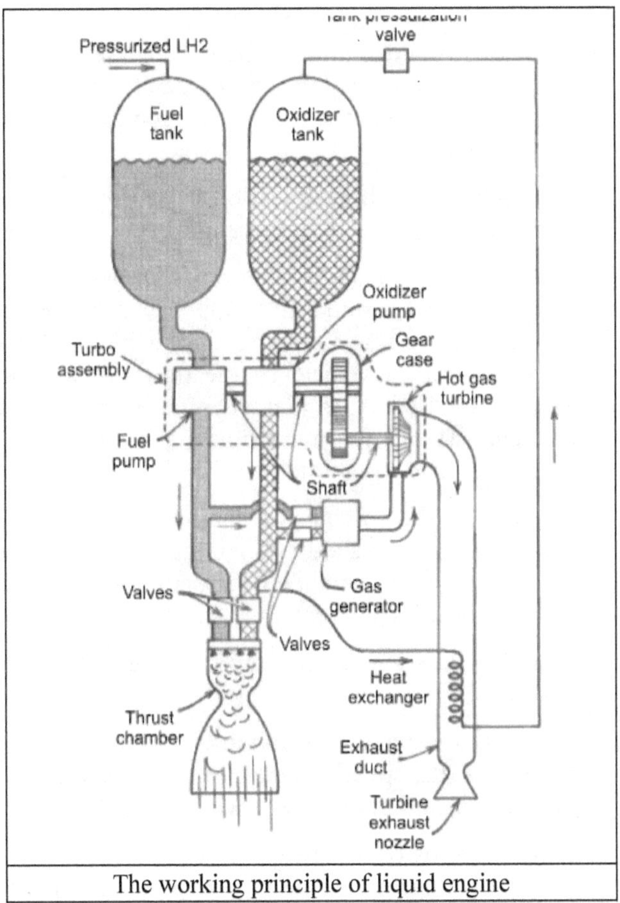

The working principle of liquid engine

The entire cylinder is filled with solid fuel, as you have seen in the previous class. Once the fuel is ignited, the pressure will be the same throughout the cylinder. You may have noticed that the burnt gases from the pressurized motor escape through the nozzle which creates thrust. However, there is a slight difference in the functioning of liquid fuel engines.

Important parts of a liquid fuel engine include:

- Fuel and oxidizer tanks

- Combustion chamber, where fuel and oxidizer are mixed together, with a nozzle system attached for exhausting the burnt gases.

- Feeding systems that transport sufficient fuel and oxidizer from the storage tanks to the combustion chamber.

Liquid fuel and liquid oxidizer are stored separately in the tank. One large tank can be divided into two half, or two separate tanks can be made and placed one on top of the other. Then there is a system that transports the required amount of fuel and oxygen from these tanks to the combustion chamber.

Why are these pipes so big? Question raised by a student after seeing fuel transporting pipe in liquid engine.

We use half inch to two inch diameter pipes for our domestic water needs in our home. They are sufficient to supply water to all the rooms in the house that require water, such as the kitchen and bathroom. However, since the launch vehicle engine needs to generate more thrust, larger pipes are used to carry larger amounts of fuel. They are so large that they require liquid fuel and oxidizer at a volume comparable to that of water pipes that bring water to many homes.

Next, let's consider the combustion chamber. The liquid fuel and oxidizer are injected in liquid state through numerous injectors inside this combustion chamber. This allows for better mixing of fuel and oxidizer during the process of injection.

In the upcoming classes, you will learn how the fuel is ignited after it has been mixed.

My father said that when overhead tanks are built in our house, if the height is too low, the speed of water in the pipe decreases. Here how to get liquid fuel and oxidizer at such high speeds?

The pressure depends on the height of the overhead tank, as the amount of water coming out of the pipe depends on that pressure. In a liquid engine, the required inlet pressure can be created by continuously feeding a certain amount of fuel and oxidizer to the burning combustion chamber.

	Merlin	RD-180	F-1	Raptor	BE-4	RS-25
Force (Tons)	84	383	677	200	240	186
Combustion Pressure (bar)	97	257	70	270	135	206

World's Largest High-Thrust Fluid Engines and Their Fuel Details

There are several methods to supply the required amount of fuel and oxidizer to the combustion chamber in the engine. The first of these methods is pressure fed system. Insert gases like helium are kept under high pressure in small cylinders. By injecting them into a cylinder containing liquid fuel and oxidizer, a certain amount of pressure can be maintained on them even as the fuel and oxidizer are reduced. Thus, fuel and oxidizer are available at the same pressure to the combustion chamber. However, this method is only suitable for very small liquid engines.

I have seen a motor running to fill petrol and diesel at petrol stations when pumping petrol. Can we keep something similar?

Petrol and diesel are stored in underground tanks at petrol stations. Pushing the handle while pumping petrol brings it up from the bottom, activating a motor to bring the petrol up. A similar system can be found in cars and buses. However, the amount of fuel and oxidizer needed in a liquid-fuel rocket engine is much higher. Therefore, we use a larger motor to transport them in the same way.

To run this system, small amounts of liquid fuel and oxidizer are burned in a small combustion chamber called gas generator to create the required power. The pumps connected via gas generator can feed the fuel to the required quantity to the main combustion chamber. As soon as these start functioning, the main combustion chamber of the liquid engine that creates the thrust starts working.

If that's the case, is there no need to pressurize the liquid fuel tank as in the case of solid fuel?

In a liquid engine, only the burning part is kept under high pressure and heat. The fuel and oxidizer storage tanks do not require higher level of pressure. Additionally, liquid fuel is used to cool the combustion chamber. By injecting a certain amount of fuel from the inlet line into the surrounding walls of the combustion chamber, this cooling system helps prevent the combustion gases from melting the material used to design the surrounding wall, even though the temperature of the combustion gases exceeds 3000 degrees. In this way, the heated fuel from the combustion chamber can be discharged back to the combustion chamber or directly through another route.

As with solid propellant, many other substances are part of formulation other than fuel and oxidizer like bonding resin curator burn rate modifier etc. Does liquid fuel require nothing?

A liquid-fueled launch vehicle requires only fuel and oxidizer. When the oxidizer and fuel required for combustion are contained in the same liquid, they are called mono-propellants. If both are required separately, they are called bi-propellant. Additionally, depending on how we store the liquid fuel, there are many types of fuels that can be stored at normal temperatures (Earth-storable) and fuels that need to be stored in cold conditions (cryogenic propellants).

Although the fuels stored under normal conditions are highly efficient, they are subject to chemical reactions in the container they are stored in. Furthermore, there are many other issues, such as corrosion and the generation of toxic gases. Therefore, they must be stored properly.

You mentioned that there are fuels which can be used in cold conditions. What is the need for this?

As I mentioned earlier, the specific impulse of a fuel varies depending on the type of fuel. To obtain a higher specific impulse, the molecular weight of the fuel should be lower. The fuels stored at the temperature of -15°C to -273°Care called cryogenic fuels.

This is why liquid hydrogen, which is a cryogenic fuel has to be stored at extreme cold temperatures of -253°C is used because it has a very low molecular weight, resulting in a high specific impulse. Liquid oxygen (-183°C) is needed to burn the hydrogen, and it must also be stored in cold conditions. Liquid methane (-161°C) is another fuel that is used in combination with liquid oxygen.

These fuels are highly energy efficient, but their storage must be kept refrigerated in order to keep them in a liquid state. The pipes used to transport these fuels must also be kept refrigerated.

You mentioned that 14.5 times more air is needed to burn the petrol in our vehicle. How much oxygen is required to burn liquid fuel?

In a liquid engine, the ratio of oxidizer to fuel is called the mixture ratio. According to chemical reactions, fuel and oxidizer must be added as per stoichiometry ratio to complete a chemical reaction. However, in order to obtain more specific impulse, lower mixture ratio also be used.

This mixture ratio varies with each fuel. It is 1.7 for typical earth storable fuels and 6 for liquid oxygen and liquid hydrogen at cryogenic temperature.

In our subject, we have read that "A fully filled pot does not spill." Like this, if more fuel is taken in the container, will it not cause disturbance to the launch vehicle?

You may have seen a milkman on a bicycle in your town. When he buys milk from the farmers, he fills the milk in three-quarters of cans or full cans. As milk is sold from house to house, the quantity decreases. So when he is cycling, this less milk will slosh and create a force.

That force can sometimes cause great difficulty for cyclists. In order to reduce the force generated by sloshing, floating materials such as straw are also placed in it. Similarly, a liquid fuel storage cylinder has some system so that the sloshing effect of liquid fuel and oxidizer effect is reduced to the extent possible to the moving launch vehicle.

When you throw a half-filled water bottle upwards, did you notice where the water is?

When the bottle is in hand, the water is in the bottom most part. But surprisingly, in a thrown bottle, if the bottle decelerates, causing the inner water mass to move to the top and the water stays at the top of the bottle due to the upward force. Similarly, when the launch vehicle is going up, due to a certain acceleration and with subsequent deceleration, the liquid fuel and oxidizer will go up in the tank. Small ullage motors are activated to bring it down instantly. When motors are operated the fuel at the top will come down and will be able to flow through the feed lines.

What is the difference between solid fuel and liquid fuel?

Liquid fuel has a higher specific impulse than solid fuel. Here, the combustion chamber is separate, so it is very easy to divert the combustion gases in the desired direction. We can keep the pressure constant. It is also easy to start and stop the engine by stopping the fuel when necessary. Not all engine require an ignition system.

Some engines spontaneously ignite as soon as the fuel and oxidizer come into contact. So the engine can be stopped and then started any number of times. Because the fuel is in liquid form, the heat generated in the combustion chamber can be controlled by fuel itself, making it much easier to use liquid engines over and over again after refurbishment.

The force generated by the moving fluid, when the speed of a lorry carrying water or liquid substances is impeded by them.

The toxicity of some fuels and the chemical reaction buildup in the tank that stores them can cause great difficulty. A liquid engine requires more parts than a solid motor, including challenging systems such as feeding pipes, pressure regulators, cooling pipe line and fuel pumps etc.

As humans are more likely to set foot on Mars, liquid engines that can use liquid oxygen and liquid methane to return to Earth using the abundant methane on Mars have been designed and those engines are now in use. Although liquid hydrogen-powered engines are more powerful, hydrogen have very low density which demand huge storage tanks for its storage. As the size of the tanks increases, the inert mass of the stage also increase.

Semi-cryo propellants are the best option based on their Isp and ease of storage of fuel. In these engines type of kerosene called rocket propellant RP-1 fueled with liquid oxygen are used in launch vehicles around the world today.

In addition to the solid and liquid fuels mentioned in the previous chapters, engines that are a mixture of the two are also being researched. "They are designed so that the fuel is generally solid, and the required oxygen is stored in liquid form and injected into the cylinder containing the solid fuel for a chemical reaction to occur."

"Every object needs energy to perform work, including you and me". Can you tell us how and in what condition we get it ? A student puzzled that.

They went to eat food while laughing and saying, 'What's so surprising about that? Rice, which is a solid substance, juice, which is a liquid substance, and payasam, which is somewhere in between the two, serve as fuel for our bodies.'

6
Nozzle

Why does the rocket spew flames from its bottom when it goes up?

As discussed in previous classes, an object needs a propulsive force to move it forward. We obtain that thrust by burning fuel to create hot gas. Instead of simply burning the fuel and releasing the resulting gases through an opening, we can achieve higher thrust by first increasing the velocity of the gases to the speed of sound and then expanding them to supersonic speeds.

When I push something, I feel the same push back. Same way, if I push out large mass of gas, I get propulsion as reaction. Push out large mass of gas means, I need to increase the rate at which mass is pushed out, which is nothing but the velocity of the gas. To increase the velocity, just like our garden hose having a conical end, we use a nozzle shape, having a shape designed to keep increasing the velocity. This shape is typically similar to two-cones attached back-to-back, converging and then diverging. Hence, it is usually called convergent-divergent nozzle.

To increase the thrust force, the exit attached to the rocket i.e. nozzle goes from a larger diameter to a smaller diameter and then increases in diameter again. This system was developed by person called de Laval, and these nozzles are called de Laval nozzle. Which has three parts namely convergent, middle narrow part called throat and exit expanding portion called divergent. As the gases travel through the narrow part of the nozzle, their speed becomes equal to the speed of sound.

According to the law of energy, "Energy can neither be created nor destroyed, only altered in form.

Combustion of fuel in a chamber produces high-temperature and high-pressure combustion gases. The energy in these gases is their excessive heat and high pressure. To convert this into the thrust we need, we have to make these gases come out through the nozzle at a high speed, and the system at the bottom of the rocket is designed to do the job perfectly. As the gas exits the engine in this way, its speed is three to five times the speed of sound.

Have you ever visited a two-wheeler or car cleaning service center? There you can see how the high-velocity water jet is used to remove soil, mud, and dirt from the vehicle. This is done by either using water from an overhead tank or by using an electric motor to increase the velocity of the water coming out of a narrow-diameter tube at the end. A similar principle is applied in rocket nozzles.

The flame on a gas stove in the house burning blue and yellow. The yellow burning fire is something that is not fully burning, and to fix it, we need to clean the top of the gas stove. But when we look at different types of rockets, the flames coming from them are different in color. Why is that?

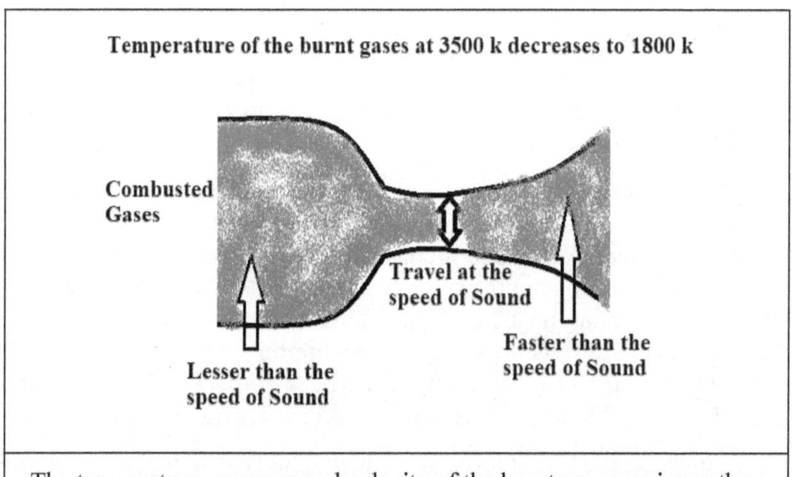

The temperature, pressure and velocity of the burnt gases varies as they pass through the nozzle.

Before we get to the previous question, could you answer the following: "Is a yellow-burning gas stove well, or is a blue-burning gas stove better?"

One student raised her hand enthusiastically and said the following:

"An uncle who visited our home last time to check the gas stove said that blue is the best color. If the gas stove burns in a yellow color, it means that the gas is not completely burnt and will run out soon. Therefore, the burner of the stove should be cleaned. I saw the blue flame after he cleaned it."

"Good, you understood very well."

Depending on the fuel used in a rocket, the color of the flame emitted from the nozzle will vary. Generally, we can see that rockets made of solid materials emit a flame of one color, while rockets made of liquid materials emit a different color. When these flames are in the rocket chamber, their temperature is more than 3000 degrees Celsius.

"That seems like an extremely high temperature. Our body temperature is only 37 degrees Celsius. Is it really one hundred times hotter?"

Thermal shields prevent the heat from the combustion gas from harming the rocket's components, especially the nozzle. The nozzle converts the energy in the high-temperature, high-pressure burnt gases into kinetic energy and expels it many times faster than the speed of sound. This part is designed to ensure that the temperature of the combustion gases coming out of it is less than 2000 degrees and its pressure is equal to the atmosphere in which the rocket operates.

As the rocket ascends, the amount of air around it decreases, leading to a decrease in atmospheric pressure. The atmospheric pressure at the top of the coast, equal to 1.01325 bar, is only 33 percent of what it is at the top of Mount Everest. Therefore, the rocket nozzle is designed with the atmospheric altitude in mind, and the pressure of the exhaust gases coming out of it is slightly lower or higher than atmospheric pressure. This design allows us to make full use of the energy available from the exhaust gases and propel the rocket forward.

Our throat also has a narrow tube through which air and food travel before reaching our stomach. Humans are able to create sound depending on how we use it. Similarly, each animal and bird produces its unique sound. Just as the air coming out of a flute can make many different sounds when it is trapped and released through a small opening, we also produce various vibration and sounds.

That's exactly right. Iron items in our homes melt at 1500 degrees and turn into liquid. These gases exist at twice that temperature. Hence, internal Thermal Protection System (TPS) should be provided to protect nozzle components. These TPS are made of heat-resilient materials or materials that are unaffected by heat.

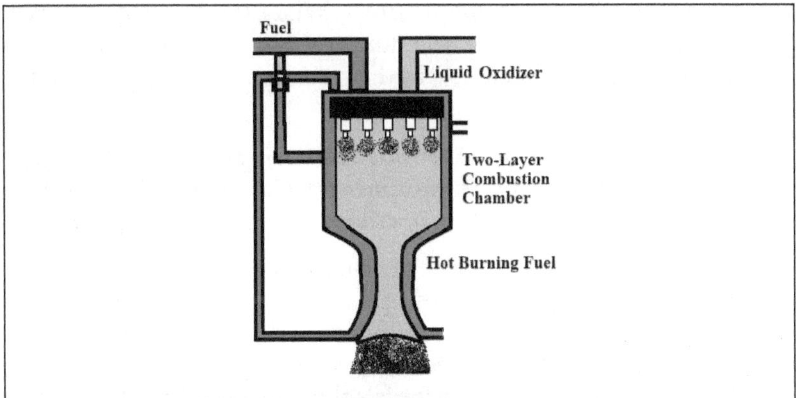

Regenerative cooling system used in the liquid engine. The circulated fuel reduces the heat generated in the walls of the combustion chamber and nozzles and heated fuel used back.

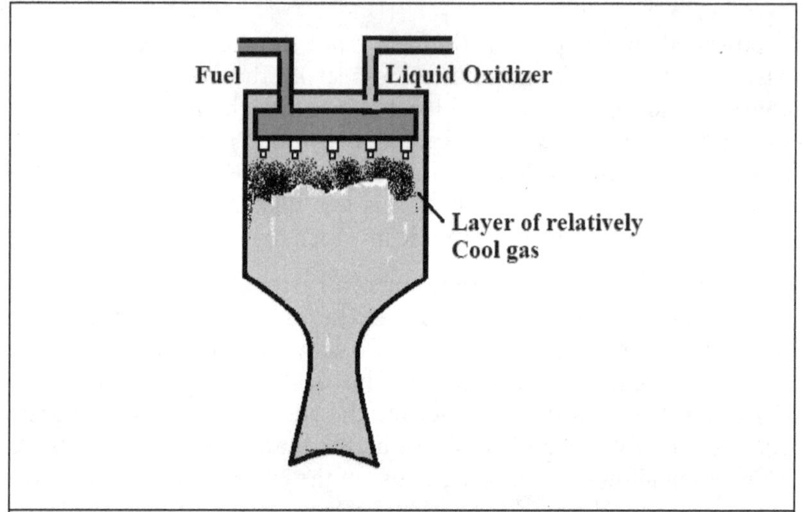

Film cooling methodology in combustion chamber. The part of fuel is sprayed on the walls of the chamber then moved towards the nozzle walls

At the end, the burnt gases are arranged to exit through a nozzle. As mentioned earlier, instead of directly releasing these gases from the combustion chamber, they are discharged through the convergent divergent nozzle system. Although the heat of a substance is expressed in degrees Celsius, its heat intensity is measured by calculating how much heat is exposed per square centimeter which is called heat flux.

So, wouldn't there be more heat when the surface area decreases?

For example, sunlight has heat flux of 600-750 watts per square meter, which is twice as much energy as solar cells mounted on a low-orbit orbit satellite (up to 1400 w/m^2). When the burnt gases reach the nozzle throat region, the heat flux level are 10,000 to 15,000 times greater than the heat flux received by sunlight during peak of the summer.

You mentioned that iron materials can melt and turn into liquid under the combustion gas environment. So, what materials are used to make the TPS, and how does it withstand such high temperatures?

The materials used to make the nozzle TPS are specific to each nozzle design. The process of turning a solid material directly into gases stage by applying extreme heat and pressure is called sublimation, and materials in TPS can be in three states: solid, liquid, and gaseous. The TPS is made of heat-resilient materials that can withstand the extreme temperatures and protect the rocket's components. It is a general rule that substances can be changed from a liquid state to a gas state by applying heat. However, there are some substances that can go directly from the solid state to the gaseous state, without passing through the liquid phase. Camphor, which is commonly used for Pooja at home, is one such substance.

You could have seen some magicians burning their hand or some rupee notes, and it seems to be unaffected. For this, they usually dip their hand or rupee note in water, before applying some alcohol and burning the same. The water takes the heat of burning, evaporates and removes the heat, thereby protecting the magician's hand or the rupee note.

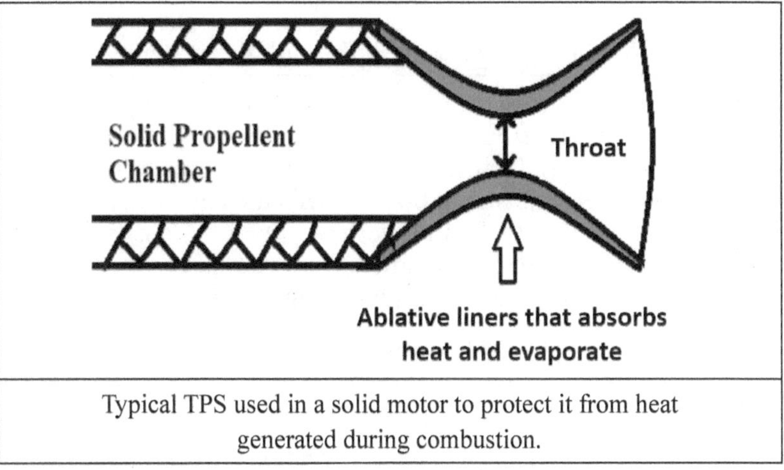

Typical TPS used in a solid motor to protect it from heat generated during combustion.

A TPS system that vaporizes when heat fallen on them to protects the surface behind it from heat called ablative materials. It is typically used in the solid motor nozzles. When ablative liners evaporates it carry the heat along with them. This process of ablation ensures drive away the instant heat fallen on the nozzle surface.

Another system used in the nozzle of a liquid engine involves absorbing heat with the fuel used, injecting liquid fuel around the backside of the metal part to absorb heat transferred to the metal.

The fuel heated in this way generates a small amount of thrust when ejected through a small hole. If not used, it goes back to the combustor where it mixes with the rocket's oxygen and fuel, which is the second method.

The third method involves a material retaining a certain amount of heat when exposed to it. When it exceeds that level, it transfers to the atmosphere, so the heated metal is not affected. This is called radiation heat transfer.

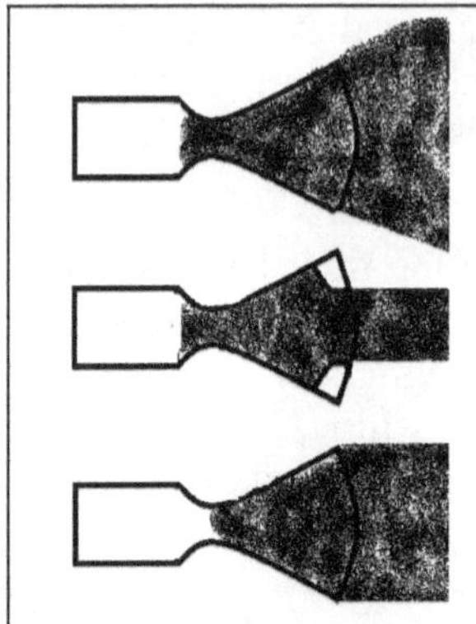

	When the released gases are at higher than atmospheric pressure
	Atmospheric air tries to move inwards as the outgoing gases pressure fall below atmospheric pressure
	When gases escape at a same pressure of the air in the atmosphere
As the burnt gases exit through the nozzle	

Because the surface of the Sun is hotter than 6000 degrees, we are 15 crore kilometers away from it and we receive sunlight in the range of 30 to 40 degrees Celsius. Radiation is one method of transferring energy from a distance. A similar method is implemented in the nozzle, where a metal in an ideal state does its work as a solid by transferring heat to the surrounding vacuum or atmosphere instead of absorbing and melting when it reaches a temperature it can tolerate.

Rather than exhausting the gases directly from the chamber, burnt gases passes the through the nozzle system adds 40 to 60 percent of the additional thrust.

The TPS of the nozzle plays an important role in determining how long an engine will function. In solid motors, the thickness of the TPS depends on the duration of operation. Long-running solid motor require a greater thickness of nozzle TPS, which increases its weight. Therefore, even the high-powered solid motors seen in previous classes are designed to run for only about two minutes.

But, at the same time, the nozzle of liquid engines has different TPS system namely regenerative cooling, radiative cooling and transpiration cooling etc. This TPS system enables liquid engines can be operated for several minutes.

Analogously, the design of the nozzle for solid and liquid engines can be compared to the process of producing light from camphor. When camphor is ignited to produce light, the camphor burns out quickly. However, if camphor is repeatedly added, light can be produced continuously. On the other hand, when oil is poured into a lamp, the wick remains intact when enough oil is available, and light is produced continuously.

7

The Spark

The students have arrived at the next campus to see how liquid engines are made. As soon as they heard the name "Spark," they got excited. They quipped that a spark is a small trap used to start a fire, and it's wonderful. The scientist from the department, who looked gigantic, came and took the matchbox there and asked who could burn these dry leaves. A student came and rubbed the matchstick, saying, "I will try it," but the first attempt ended in failure. The next attempt also failed.

He said, "I think I couldn't burn it because the leaves were a bit wet. Well, let me give you some waste papers. Try and see if you can burn them."

Taking the waste paper and burning it with a matchstick and keeping the leaves on top of each other, they started burning all the leaves. He raised the question, "Is it a burning object?" just by pointing out the nearby firewood. Some students said that firewood is definitely a fuel hence burning object, and they learned in the first class that one kilogram of firewood requires seven to eight kilograms of oxygen.

He raised the question, "Yes, who can explain the relation between coal and firewood?" A girl said, "We have seen coal being extracted from the mine when we went on a trip to Neyveli." A boy explained that "coal is formed when forests and mountains are buried underneath and exposed to high pressure and temperature for over the millions of years".

Another girl shared the story from her village and said that "In our village, villagers cut the trees that grow as hedges, cut them into pieces, burn them for a while, and after removing the moisture from them, they sell them as charcoal. As the moisture in the wood is removed, the charcoal is more energy-efficient. I have seen it being used for heating by putting it inside a non-electric iron to remove the wrinkles of the clothes.

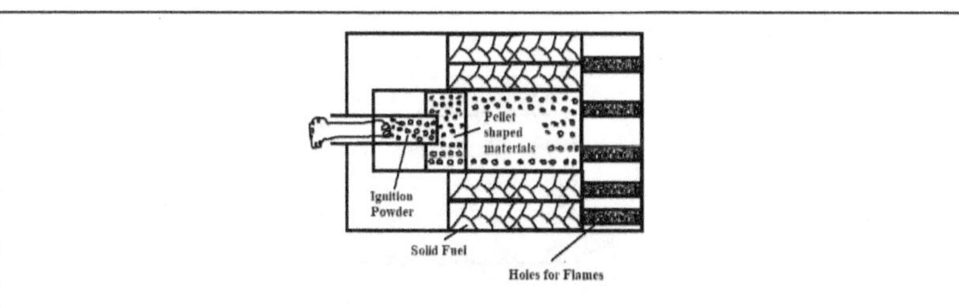

The method of filling the fuel mixture used to ignite the launch vehicle from an electric spark

Hydrogen, carbon, and hydrocarbon qualify as fuels, but the difficulty lies in burning them. The wood that you are looking at now cannot be lit with a matchstick and paper, but it can be ignited by pouring kerosene on it and lighting it.

He took them to the facility where ignition systems are made for rocket engines, saying, "You are going to see here how the solid motor and liquid engines you have seen in the previous classes are ignited."

"Our two-wheeler starts when my father kicks it," he said. "With the energy generated during kicking, a spark ignites the mixture of petrol and air entering the engine. He also told me that batteries are used to create a similar spark in a car. Is this how we ignite the launch vehicle engines?"

"Good question. We haven't gone in yet," he eagerly replied, "but I will answer all these doubts."

You might have heard that "little drops of water make a mighty ocean," just like how big a rocket engine needs to be ignited, it starts with a small spark. A launch vehicle will need electricity for a variety of applications, including creating a spark. A small spark is first created in this ignition system, which initiates the burning of fuel in powder form.

To ignite a Diwali firecracker or rocket, begin by placing a small flame from a blowtorch onto the wick located at the tip of the cracker. The wick, once lit, steadily burns, allowing the explosive substance within the cracker to ignite. As the fire spreads through the wick, the cracker will ignite and explode, shooting upwards in a dazzling display.

Similarly, these powders can ignite the next-stage burning material contained in the pellets, which are enclosed in a cavity comprising holes, which act like small nozzles. For a small solid fuel engine, these pelletized fuels, once ignited, allow the flame to pass through the holes and spread to all parts of the solid fuel to ignite the solid fuel cylinder.

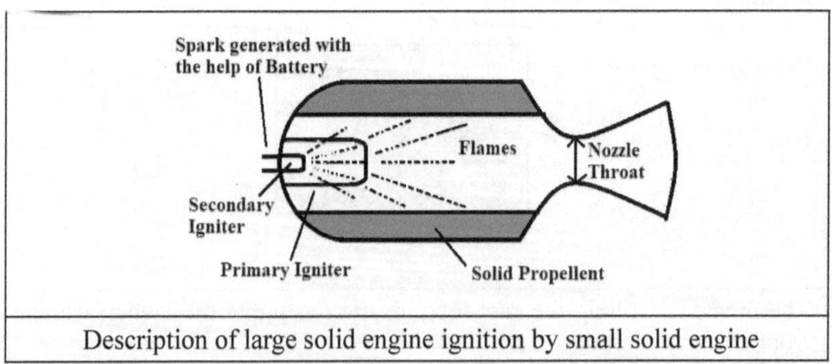

Description of large solid engine ignition by small solid engine

Do large engines also use this method of ignition?

The difference between the time we give the spark and the time it takes for the entire engine to start burning is called ignition delay. If enough energy is not given, only some parts of the solid fuel will start to burn, while others remain unlit. Therefore, a small igniter made of solid fuel takes the fire from a pellet-like material to ignite the long and heavy solid fuel.

Depending on the length and diameter of the motor, sometimes a single igniter is not sufficient. In that case, a small solid motor called secondary igniter is first ignited, which then ignites the larger primary igniter, for Facilitating the motor ignition.

and then the entire solid motor is ignited from it.

Only if this igniter is fixed more than half a percent of the length of the cylinder filled with a solid motor, there is a chance that the flame will reach all parts of the cylinder. A solid fuel engine used for this kind of ignition is provided with many small holes for the fire to escape and reach various parts. Each of those holes is placed in a different location and viewing angle in the solid propellant inside the motor.

A student from a village asked, "When I light a wood-burning stove at home, it catches fire immediately. But during the rainy season, it catches fire a bit slowly. I don't understand why you say ignition delay is the main factor when fuel catches fire slowly.

As soon as the command to generate the spark is given, all the above actions take place one after the other to generate thrust throughout the entire solid motor in the blink of an eye. The time difference between these two actions should be between 300 milliseconds to 1,000 milliseconds; otherwise, the energy of the fuel will be wasted without achieving the desired thrust. To ensure this, the holes in the igniter are designed accordingly.

Additionally, when the pressure inside the solid motor increases, the speed of spark propagation also increases. Therefore, the nozzle of the solid rocket is sealed with a closure. Once all the fuel has ignited and the pressure has increased to five to ten bar pressure, this barrier breaks, and the engine begins to deliver thrust. This action is similar to 'closure/corks' used in medicine bottles or similar items, which needs a minimum force to break open, and hence avoiding accidental opening by kids.

Some launch vehicles have several smaller engines around them to assist the booster when it takes off from ground. These can range from 2 to 6 and are named as strapon motors. If the motors in the opposite direction do not start at the same time, it will result in a difference in the thrust generated by them at different instances which may create a side force pushing the launch vehicle to one side. To limit this the ignition of strapons shall be in a controlled way.

A boy raised a question by pointing to the name board which read "liquid fuel that burns automatically when touched". "I have seen my grandmother suffered like this while cooking on the wood stove at home. But in a kerosene stove, it is very easy to make a fire with a matchstick, and in a gas stove with a small ignition lighter. Are the ignition tools you have mentioned here required for liquid fuel as well?"

Generally, two types of liquid fuels are used, one is stored at room temperature, and the other is cryogenic fuel storage, which requires extremely low temperatures. Liquid fuels and oxidizers that are stored at room temperature usually ignite spontaneously upon contact and do not require an ignition system. These types of fuels are also preferred for generating thrust by stopping and restarting the engine multiple times.

However, certain liquid fuels may require an ignition system for combustion, depending on their chemical composition and storage conditions. For example, some fuels may be highly volatile and require a spark to ignite, while others may need to be heated before they can ignite. The specific ignition tool used will depend on the type of fuel and the conditions under which it is stored and used.

In summary, while not all liquid fuels require an ignition system, certain types may need it depending on their chemical composition and storage conditions.

Once a solid fuel is ignited, it burns completely and then stops. Therefore, it is not possible to start and stop. Similarly, cryogenic fuels require a spark to ignite. A small igniter capable of delivering heat energy for up to three seconds is used in a liquid engine like this. When fuel and oxygen are pumped through multiple holes and ignited in one spot, the entire combustion chamber ignites within milliseconds.

If non-auto-ignitable liquid fuels, such as cryogenics, need to be repeatedly ignited, systems capable of producing a spark at multiple time must be provided, which is similar to the petrol or diesel engine requirement in our bikes and cars.

The ignition delay plays an important role here, as you mentioned earlier?

Suppose a boy is trying to light the gas stove in your house. He turns on the knob of the gas stove, but because he doesn't know how to properly light the lighter in the stove burner, he is just playing with it in the kitchen. What happens after a few seconds?

A girl recalls a similar experience, saying, "It's a great story. Such an incident happened in my life, but I had a narrow escape from it.

One day, I opened the knob and took out a non-working lighter and pressed it for four or five seconds. Then, realizing it didn't work, I lit a matchstick. Suddenly, a big fire broke out in the kitchen as the gas had filled around the stove. I was very much scared."

Similarly, could this happen in the combustion chamber of a liquid engine?

Yes, certainly, there is a similar possibility in the combustion chamber. That's why when liquid fuel is ignited, only a small percentage of the amount of fuel needed to produce full thrust is initially injected into the combustion chamber. If the ignition time is increased for any reason, excess fuel will reach the combustion chamber.

With a delayed spark, all the excess fuel will suddenly catch fire and start burning, generating excessive heat in the combustion chamber. This can cause the combustion chamber and its related parts to melt and fail due to the excessive heat, leading to engine malfunction.

Normally, we take many precautions to keep the gas stoves used in our homes safe. In the same way, how are these engine ignition systems and spark generators protected?

Typically, solid motor is not equipped with spark-generating systems when they are transported from one location to another, as a spark could cause massive damage. These ignition systems are attached to the motor only when it is on the launch pad.

Additionally, a system capable of generating a spark with energy from a battery is provided with safety mechanisms to prevent the spark from entering the engine. Minutes before the launch vehicle lifts off, the engines are turned by an automatic electric motor to face the direction of ignition.

You saw a small solid engine that helps to ignite a big solid motor and said that this is also a solid motor. Is there any difference between the two?

Typically, a solid motor fuel used in a launch vehicle will have up to 20 percent fuel such as aluminum in the powdered form to increase its temperature. This is done to raise the temperature of gases produced by chemical reactions. However, small solid motor that ignite a main solid motor need to burn faster once initiate.

Materials containing high amounts of oxidizer are added to increase their burning speed. For pyrogen igniter that help to ignite a solid motor, it is important how fast they burn compared to the temperature of their burnt gas. Therefore, igniter are designed to produce a high-speed spark with high power and low energy.

The scientist pointed out to the student that great leaders have said that a small incident can change one's life. The student had read in Mahatma Gandhi's biography that he was a changed person after he listened to Harichandra's drama and decided to speak only the truth.

As I looked around the campus, it became clear that the first step in the journey of a launch vehicle for launch was to create a spark. In the next class, it was discussed that without this spark, a large engine cannot provide its driving force.

8
Multistage launch vehicle

Everyone was eagerly waiting after a mind sparking classes to learn the secrets of how the stages of rockets are made.

Multi-stage models of the launch vehicle were placed side by side to understand the construction of the launch vehicle. Not only the liquid engine that the students had seen earlier, but also each stage was equipped with engines. They also had a system for transferring thrust from the engine to the launch vehicle.

In addition to that, many modules were assembled in each launch vehicle stage, such as shields to protect from heat, tanks for storing liquid fuel, facilities for Gimballing of combustion chamber of liquid engines, flexing solid motor nozzles as needed, assembly parts to help joining, and products carrying different sensors that can observe the various physical and thermal condition of the launch vehicle.

Everyone was instructed to take models of the launch vehicle stages and try to assemble as a complete launch vehicle by themselves. Students assembled different launch vehicles by combining the launch vehicle stages and the structure that fit into the next stage.

The activity, which was like a puzzle game, excited the students and helped them understand how the launch vehicle was put together step by step. A particular stage was designed to be attached to that particular model of the vehicle only, so they searched and found the next stage after the first stage they received.

"What is this? A 2-stage launcher and a 4-stage launcher are kept here. I have a 5-stage launch vehicle," one student said. The expert in that field arrived to explain it at the moment when the doubt arose in their minds as to why there was such a decrease and increase in the number of stages.

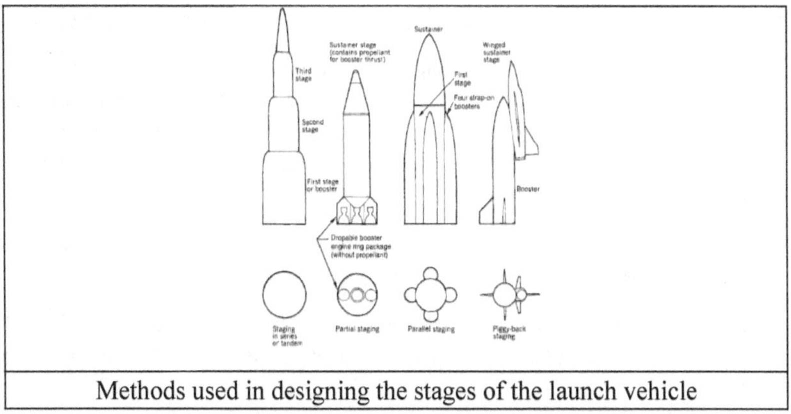

Methods used in designing the stages of the launch vehicle

In the previous classes, you have learned about how a liquid engine and solid motor are constructed. However, it is not enough to simply create the engine. It must also be modified to make it useful for the launch vehicle.

For example, think about a car or bus that we see on the road. The engine is a system that is used to propel the vehicle forward. The force generated by the engine is transferred to the wheels, which allows them to rotate.

A vehicle is only considered complete when all the necessary systems are combined, including the fuel tank, provisions for storing items needed for travel, systems for transferring the force generated by the engine to the wheels, and the wheels themselves for movement.

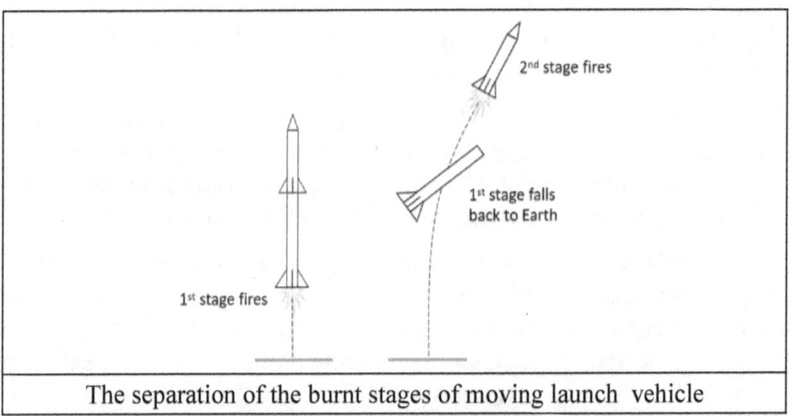

The separation of the burnt stages of moving launch vehicle

In a racing car design, only the driver sits whereas in a normal car designed for family travel includes seats for everyone, a audio system for listening to music, and a LED screen for monitoring several parameters during travel are required.

Similarly, the stages of a launch vehicle are designed by fitting necessary components after the launch vehicle engine has been decided.

A student once questioned, while holding a model of a launch vehicle, "We made a two-stage launch vehicle out of these launch vehicles. A five-stage launch vehicle was also made by my friend. Why do the number of stages vary? We don't really understand its significance."

There are many subsystems in a launch vehicle, along with the propellant, storage tanks, control mechanisms etc.

As spacecraft carried by the launch vehicle move towards the specified orbit. Stored fuel is consumed to carry the used launch vehicle stages with them. Thus, each stage will be separated from the launch vehicle as soon as it has completed its burn time successfully. Launch vehicles typically have single-use engines and stages.

To illustrate, let's assume we participate in a mountaineering competition where we can only reach the top of the mountain after ten days of climbing. The weight of the spacecraft carried by the launch vehicle can be considered as the weight of our body. Food is vital to provide us with the energy we need to climb, and we must carry water and necessary food in different containers and walk with necessary items for 10 days.

There will be no one to help and no way to purchase food on the mountain, so we must carry the necessary items ourselves. Understand that climbing the mountain is a significant challenge, so it's crucial to reduce weight while climbing.

We begin this story by noting that you weigh 50 kg while traveling, but when you add water and food for ten days, your total weight becomes 100 kg. Of the remaining 50 kg, only 40 kg of food items are packed, while the containers holding them weigh 10 kg. Since there's no use in carrying empty containers after we've eaten our food each day, we leave them one by one when we come to places where we can dispose off garbage. When we finally reach the top of the mountain, you're the only one who weighs 50 kg.

This is how a launch vehicle continues its journey. However, the difference here is that if a 400-ton launch vehicle takes off, the satellite or spacecraft that will eventually land in orbit will weigh less than 10 tons in lower earth orbit.

In the above story, we mention that the ratio between the weight of food items and the total weight after packing them in containers is called the mass ratio. The weight ratio of each stage in the launch vehicle represents the ratio of the weight of fuel filled in that stage to the total weight of that stage.

Increasing this ratio indicates that the launch vehicle's design have been optimized, and unnecessary weight has been reduced. We can imagine packing many dress items with lightweight bags on our tour. Typically, this weight ratio varies from 80 percent to 93 percent for different launch vehicle stage.

If the launch vehicle takes off from the ground and passes through dense air and reaches to space where no air present, then a low-thrust engine will be sufficient. Carrying unnecessary items is a wastage of energy.

If we have to go on a tour, the travel will be comfortable only if we go with less luggage. Otherwise, we would struggle to load and unload our bags at railway station. There won't be enough space in the bus to store the luggage, and we would find it hard to carry it up to our rooms in the hostels. Similarly, to travel without any difficulties, the stages attached to the launch vehicle are removed one by one, and only the remaining part goes into the space.

Oh, so are you saying that a launch vehicle with more stages is better?

Actually, if the launch vehicle is designed with multiple stages, the total weight required to lift off from Earth will be reduced. But the problem is that the more stages a vehicle has, the more parts it has, and integrating each stage to the next requires a lot of work. This can make it difficult to assemble and launch the vehicle. Therefore, launch vehicles with a minimum of two stages and a maximum of five stages are in use today.

Can't we develop a single-stage launch vehicle?

Although it would reduce the number of items that need to be carried into space, the weight of the rocket would be significantly high due to the requirement of the first stage to generate greater thrust in order to lift the entire payload. Therefore, a launch vehicle with at least two stages is required, primarily to pass through the atmospheric air. After that, the next stage will operate until the satellite is placed on the specified circular orbit.

As you mentioned, when a small package is delivered to my house, it is first loaded onto a vehicle inside a large truck. Once the truck arrives at its destination, the package is transferred to a smaller vehicle for transport. Finally, the package is delivered to me by someone on a two-wheeler. This is similar to the concept of a launch vehicle with multiple stages.

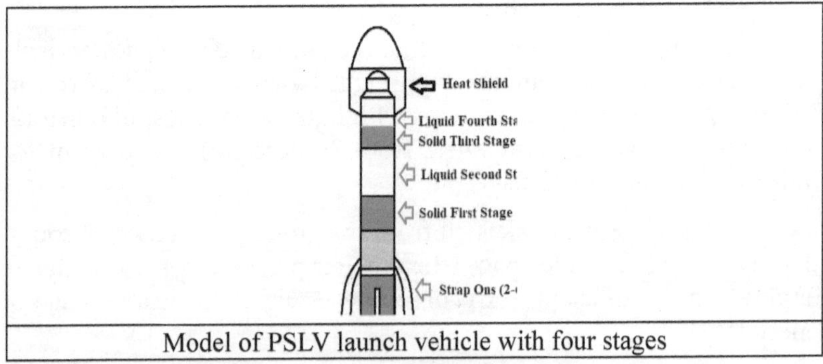

Model of PSLV launch vehicle with four stages

Your analogy is correct. The final stage, which is used to stabilize the satellite in orbit, will produce the least amount of thrust and will be made to be lightweight.

We saw that there are small strapon around the main booster stage that provide the necessary thrust when the launch vehicle takes off from the earth, and the strapons can provide additional thrust to it. Are they considered a separate stage of the launch vehicle? How are the stages of the launch vehicle named?

The names are given depending on how the thrust is obtained in the launch vehicle. Generally, when the primary stage of the launch vehicle takes off from the earth and gives thrust, small engines burning around it also give thrust. Then, we call them the zeroth stage. But if the primary engine does not fire, and the starpons around the first stage start giving the primary thrust after the first burnout, then they are called stage 1 and stage 2.

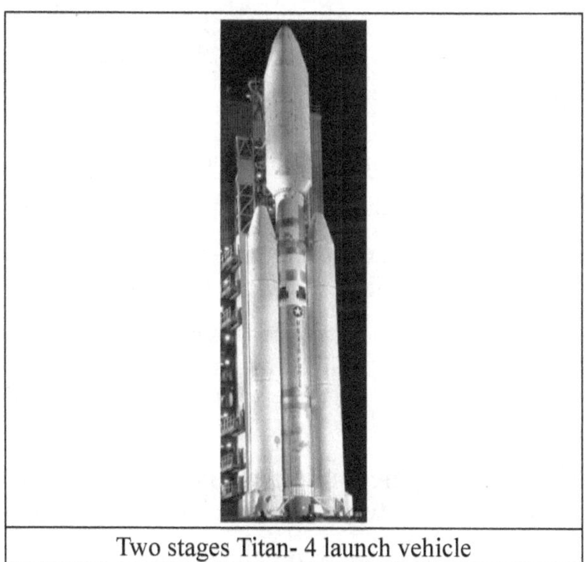

Two stages Titan- 4 launch vehicle

What are the tiny little motors attached to each stage of the launch vehicle like?

When the launch vehicle moves forward and a stage has finished burning, the spend off stage must be separated. However, there is a problem: the launch vehicle and the stage to be removed are traveling at the same speed.

When moving objects that are separated in unequal proportions, the lighter object will travel at a greater speed than the heavier object.

When we remove the lighter, burnt stage, it will try to travel faster than the launch vehicle. Attempting such travel would leave it vulnerable to collision with other parts of the moving launch vehicle.

To avoid collisions, small retro motors are equipped for pulling in a different direction. They run for only one or two seconds and safely remove the burnt-out stages without hitting the launch vehicle.

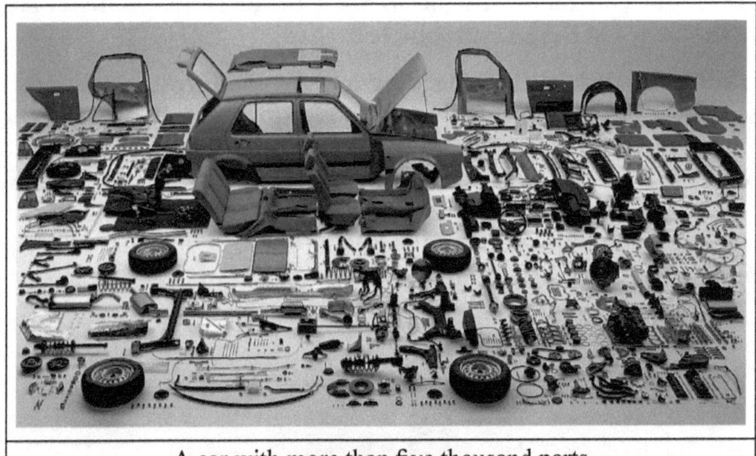

A car with more than five thousand parts

Is it possible to count the number of parts in a launch vehicle?

Take a pen in your hand to understand this. Let's see how many parts you can divide a pen into and count them.

Then, a girl gets up and points out that a pen has ten parts, including a small tube that stores ink, an iron structure (nib) at the end, an outer structure to hold it, systems to connect it up and down, and a cap to keep it closed.

Similarly, if you imagine your bicycle, how many parts are there in it? Only the spokes on the two wheels of a bicycle are more than 50.

Likewise, a two-wheeler has more than a thousand parts, and a car has more than five thousand parts. Just as there are many single spokes in a bicycle, there are many systems, such as fasteners, that help connect the parts of a rocket. Launch vehicles are made of over a lakh materials. All these materials are carefully assembled to form a complete launch vehicle. If an item or component does not work for some reason, it can cause the launch vehicle to fail.

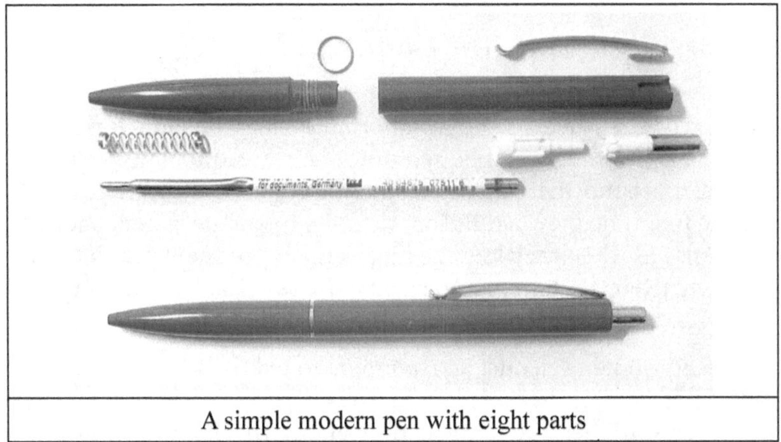

A simple modern pen with eight parts

Several instruments have been used to predict "How is the health of the launch vehicle? Is it going as far as it should go?" These devices are connected with electrical wires, similar to how our houses are connected. Kilometers of electrical wires can be seen on a large launch vehicle. A computer system is mounted on its head to monitor the entire operation of the launch vehicle. It reports each and every activity of the launch vehicle to the ground control station.

The students worked to explore the similarities and differences between the various launch vehicle components. They also learned that in the coming classes, they will discover how the launch vehicle's speed and trajectory are determined.

9

The Launch pad

Everyone reached the next important area - the launch pad from which launch vehicles can be sent into the sky. Although the students had been around the launch campus throughout their training, this was the first time they had the opportunity to see the launch pad. They were amazed when they saw the huge launch pedestal built to support the launch vehicle standing up against the sky. The bus carrying them was parked near the pedestal, making it look like a toy.

A bold women scientist arrived there to tell the story of the launch pad. After hearing her, explain various aspects of launch, everyone loudly agreed that the information about the launch vehicle was amazing and wonderful. She asked, "What did you think about the need for a launch pad, from what you have seen so far?"

A boy said, "I think a launch pad is needed for launch vehicles to lift off, just like how a bus needs a bus stand to rest and depart, a train needs a railway station to pick up passengers, and an airport and runway is needed for an airplane to take off."

In the nineteenth century, the invention of crude oil led to the production of petrol and diesel engines, which were used to manufacture cars. Airplanes were also made and started flying, while early attempts were made to develop a liquid-fueled flying object. As you may have learned in the previous class, Goddard was the first to succeed in this technology.

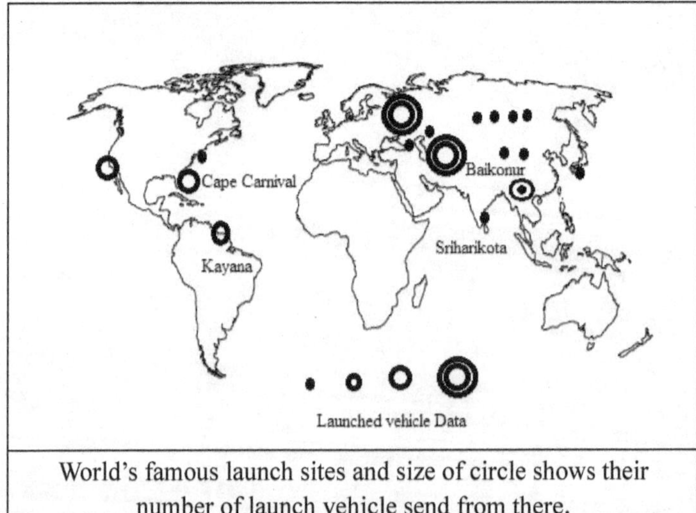

World's famous launch sites and size of circle shows their number of launch vehicle send from there.

Next, there was the development of liquid-fueled missiles. The main reasons for this were that solid fuel technology was not yet developed, and the chances of accidents during solid fuel production were high. Hitler used liquid fuel to make missiles for his army, and his V-2 missile was prepared with liquid ethanol and liquid oxygen.

It was ten years after the end of World War II that solid propellant missiles entered the US military. Launching liquid-fueled missiles required first filling the tanks with fuel, which took a long time - ranging from 10 to 30 minutes depending on the size of the missile. During refueling, the launch pad was vulnerable to attack and could face heavy damage. To mitigate this, bunkers were set up and filled with liquid fuels, and faster-filling designs were developed.

So, do we call the launch pad the place that is set up to hold the launch vehicle?

The place where everything needed to prepare the launch vehicle is available called the launch pad complex. Small launchers and missiles can be launched from a lift-off platform, but launching heavier launch vehicles requires a dedicated launch pad and more space.

When we arrived at this launch campus, we got off at the railway station and traveled a long distance by bus. No residential areas could be found in between. Why was this launch campus set up so far away?

A launch vehicle uses tons of fuel, and if it explodes due to unforeseen reasons during takeoff, there is a great chance that it will fall in a residential area, causing severe causalities. Therefore, launch pads are usually set up on islands and deserts where there are no residential areas. Once the launch vehicle takes off to space, its path will be designed in such a way that it travels above the ocean.

Upon entering the campus, we saw a name board stating that we were near the equator. Is there a reason for that?

In the solar system, the Earth rotates on its own axis, an imaginary line that passes through poles, and revolves around the Sun. It takes 24 hours for the Earth to complete one rotation. Since the Earth is nearly spherical, the equatorial region is the thick line in the middle of the Earth that divides it into two parts. The velocity at the surface of the Earth is greater in the equatorial region, than at other latitudes or poles.

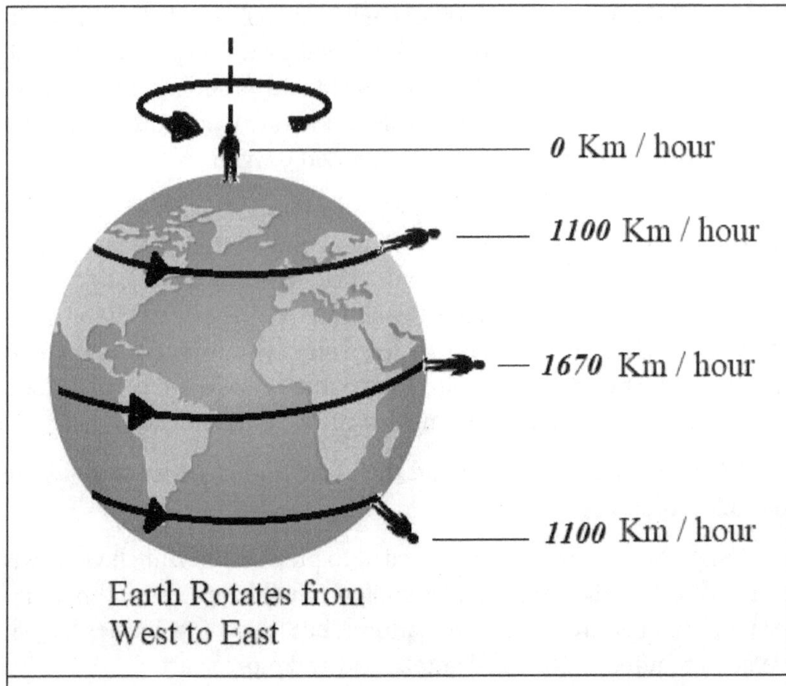

The speed of the ground felt at different points on the surface of the earth even though the earth rotates once every twenty-four hours.

For example, consider the globe. At the top, the distance to go around the pole (ie circumference) near the pole is much shorter than the distance to go around the equator. Similarly, even though the Earth rotates at the same angular speed (degrees/radians per second), a person standing at the poles will be traveling at a slower linear speed (meters per second) and a person above the equator will be traveling at a higher linear speed.

So near the equator the speed of the earth is 460 meters per second. When we launch a satellite, to keep it in a certain orbit without falling down due to gravitation pull of earth, its speed should be varied with its altitude. If the satellite is to be stationary at an altitude of thirty-six thousand kilometers, it is required to rotate at a speed of three kilometers per second. It would have to travel at a speed of 7.35 kilometers per second at around thousand kilometers from Earth.

The launch pad is placed as close to the equator as possible so that it is useful to take off from near the equator in order to give the object the momentum we have on Earth. Suppose a person traveling in a bus gets off the bus before the bus stops, he will be pushed forward due to the momentum gained when he was inside the bus. We can interpret this as the momentum of the bus pushing him forward as he disembarks.

All the rocket engines are only manufactured at the launch site?

Rocket engines can be manufactured in several areas and brought to the launch site. Since liquid engines are refueled only at the last moment, launch vehicle stages powered by lighter liquid fuel can be brought to the launch site from elsewhere. Safety issues do not arise as there is no- fuel presence.

But in solid motors, the propellant must be pre-filled. Small solid motors can be brought to the launch site from other areas. But safety measures should be strictly followed while handling them. Instead, vessels used in solid motors are prepared and brought to the launch campus where they solid propellent are caste and transported to the launch pad.

There they saw a large launch vehicle ready for launch. A boy said, "depending on the size of the launch vehicle and how many stages it has, it can take anywhere from 10 days to 30 days."

The launch vehicle assembly building, helps to stack the launch vehicle stages one after the other. When the size of the solid stage is large, it is not possible to bring them together.

NASA developed a 730-ton propellant filled solid motor for their maiden moon launch vehicle but could not use. Solid motors are usually built in multi segments with a heavier weight. They are stacked one after the other in the launch vehicle assembly building to prepare the entire vehicle. At the same time, since the liquid engine is fueled at the last moment, they are brought fully assembled to the assembly building where they are integrated with other stages.

On our way to the building where the launch vehicle is assembled, we saw several large buildings. What kind of work is being done in them?"

A bird's eye view of the launch pads set up at the Cape Carnival in the United States

As mentioned earlier, the launch site complex also includes solid motor production systems, storage facilities for liquid fuel, and transport vehicles for moving heavy launch vehicle components between locations.

Wow! With such a large launch vehicle present, was it built here or brought here directly?

The launch vehicle will be the last component to be transported to the launch pad. Before that, we will visit the buildings where the launch vehicle stages are assembled. There are three assembly buildings are there. The first stage of the launch vehicle is assembled in the first facility , while the next three stages are assembled in the next assembly bay. The solid fuel engines are stacked vertically in this assembly buildings.

"Since the liquid stages of the launch vehicle are lightweight, they are transported horizontally and then raised upright on the launch pad. However, the launch vehicle with heavy solid motor cannot be transported this way."

After all the vehicle's parts are ready, the satellite and spacecraft to be launched are attached to the upper part, and the whole vehicle is taken to the launch pad. Everyone was amazed to see a specially-made, weight-bearing vehicle that could carry a weight of a thousand tons and move on tracks. Its wheels were several feet in diameter. After the launch vehicle reaches launch pad, it will take a few days to complete the final tasks before flying towards the sky.

The pedestal you see here was originally a pillar designed to help hold the launch vehicle. This is an important aid in preventing the launch vehicle from falling down due to wind gusts. Just like when babies are in the mother's womb, the nutrients they need go from the mother's body to the baby through the umbilical cord. Similarly, the energy required for the various functions in the launch vehicle is available through the tubes hanging there.

The launch vehicle is equipped with many electronic devices that are powered by batteries provided in the launch vehicle. However, when the launch vehicle is standing on the launch pad, it uses electricity from the ground, thereby saving the energy of the batteries. The corresponding systems are on the launch pedestal.

Liquid propellants are refueled only a few hours before launch. Here, you can also find the system to fill them. Cryogenic fuels that can be stored in cold conditions will evaporate and be lost. There is also a system to compensate for that loss until the launch vehicle takes off. These systems are arranged in such a way that they are released automatically when the launch vehicle takes off.

We have seen launch vehicles take off on television, but everyone watches from a remote computer room. Why is no one near the launch pad during launch?

We have various Diwali cracker. Some you hold in hand and crack, while for some you run after keeping the spark. Launch vehicle are like these, only they are hundreds of times more dangerous to be near-by.

When the launch vehicle ejects the burnt gases and creates tremendous thrust, the sound generated by these gases is almost intolerable to our ears. So, they can only be observed from several kilometers away when the launch vehicle takes off. Normal human speaking volume is less than 100 decibels, while it can go up to 120 decibels when speaking in front of a mic during festivals. However, it will be over 150 decibels when the launch vehicle takes off. When NASA's space shuttle began its journey, it was calculated that the sound level emitted by the launch vehicle that carried it into space was up to 200 decibels.

Since this sound is energy, it can cause damage to the building where the launch vehicle is built, the launch pad, and surrounding buildings. Therefore, NASA scientists directed the gases from the large launch vehicle in a specific direction and splashed water to reduce the sound level by up to 50 decibels. We can see many such systems on the launch pad.

We need to fully monitor the each and every parameters of the launch vehicle to determine its health prior to launch as well as during the journey. For that, hundreds of sensor data will be checked one by one, and the launch vehicle will be prepared accordingly. No one is allowed to come close to the vehicle once the fueling is done.

Therefore, all these functions are executed from a remote monitoring station. After checking the stages and physical condition of the launch vehicle at each stage, it is allowed to take off.

In the past, launch pads used to be so small that other countries were not aware of them. However, Russia, which was the first to develop a space launch vehicle, established a missile base in Kazakhstan without anyone's knowledge. This remained unknown to the outside world for many years until the US noticed the launch pad with their spy airplanes.

Regarding the sequence of the world's heaviest launch vehicle supporting launch pads, the USA's Kennedy Space Center has the highest supporting facility for 3,000 tons of launch vehicle, followed by Russia's Baikonur launch pad supported upto 2,400 tons weight of a launch vehicle. China, India, and Japan launch vehicles with the heaviest weight of 880 tons, 640 tons, and 445 tons, follows in the list.

I read in the newspaper that small launch vehicles are often used for research, in addition to launch sites that launch heavier launch vehicles. What is the difference between these two types of sites?

To learn about the atmosphere, we first used balloons which filled with less dense gases. However, balloons need a certain amount of air to fly. Balloons can be used for research up to 40 km above sea level.

Research can also be done with satellites positioned at high altitudes above the Earth. These satellites need to be positioned at high orbital velocity due to the gravitational pull when they are close to the Earth. The orbital velocity reduces when altitude increases from earth surface. For example, a low-earth orbit satellite is required to orbit at 7.5 to 8 kilometers per second. Whereas a satellite orbiting at an altitude of 10,000 kilometers would be 5 kilometers per second.

However, for certain types of research, we need to keep the satellite below a height of 120 km. There is also a type of launch vehicle designed to continue research into the atmosphere-free space between 40 km and 120 km, where the density of the atmosphere has decreased. If study carried out in these altitudes where earth magnetic field lines pass through will provide enormous scientific data. The launch vehicle used to carry the payloads in these altitude are very small launch vehicles, small launch pads are set up in densely populated areas. The Thumba launch pad is the best example, which is located in Thiruvananthapuram, where the magnetic lines are passing.

This small type of launch vehicle is designed to carry and release research materials from an altitude of 50 km to 120 km. It slowly descends through a parachute-like system and travels for a few minutes until it reaches the ground where research is carried out.

These types of launch vehicles are known as sounding rockets, from the Latin word "sounde", meaning that measurements are being taken. The name "sounding rocket" is used to describe these rockets because they are designed to probe or explore the atmosphere in the regions where balloons and satellite cannot be placed. These rockets travel at approximately four times the speed of sound, creating a distinct sound as they go also.

After the day's class, everyone returned to their hostel and talked to their friends about the amazing things they had learned. One student remarked that they could now only wonder how products weighing thousands of kilos were made. They were used to buying rice, tomatoes, and okra in kilos, and sometimes their father brought home bags of rice weighing 100 kgs. However, at the launch campus facility, everything is measured in tons!

10
Shielding systems

The manager took everyone to the launch vehicle thermal protection system design area, saying that they would learn about it by observing two girls who were discussing the extreme heat and hot burnt gases that can come out of the launch vehicle at several hundred degrees. They wondered how the vehicle could be protected from such intense heat when they themselves couldn't bear even a few degrees of heat in the summer.

The scientists had a diagram showing how to calculate the heat coming from hot air. On Earth, the 700-800 w/m^2 heat flux only available from sunlight. However, solar panels mounted on satellites and space stations that are above the Earth's atmosphere receive twice as much of this.

One student raised a question, asking why they used area to describe heat intensity instead of degrees.

The scientists answered that they calculated how much heat, on average, reaches a surface area. When the same amount of heat is transferred over a smaller area, its density is greater, and when it covers a larger area, its concentration is less.

The student then understood and shared their own experience of using a magnifying glass to concentrate heat in one spot. When the glass absorbed heat from the sun, it created a small circular spot that punched a hole in their book within seconds."

A boy who makes holes in the pages of a book by focusing the heat from the sun on a single point

The heated gas generated inside the motor and combustion chamber travels through the nozzle. As you may recall from previous chapters, the burnt gases are released by accelerating them to the speed of sound and then expanding them through the nozzle.

To achieve this, the diameter of the nozzle is first reduced, which increases the velocity of the gases and, therefore, the heat concentration of the burnt gases at throat region.

When the hot burnt gases reach the throat portion of the nozzle, its heat flux can be more than 2000 W/cm^2. By the time the gases exit through the nozzle and reach the atmosphere, their velocity is four to six times the speed of sound, and their heat flux will be is 50 to 100 W/cm^2. Notably, this is a thousand times more than normal sunlight that we receive on earth.

Oh, so that's why we can't stand near the launch vehicle when it takes off? When they mentioned excessive sound in previous classes, I wondered if we could watch with our ears covered. Then I realized that even if we closed our ears, we would still be affected by the heat.

Just like burning firewood in winter, the heat concentration of these burnt gases decreases as we move away from the source. However, the launch vehicle's pedestal is subjected to this heat. To protect the pedestal components, thermal protection systems are used. The pillars supporting the launch pedestal and surrounding ironwork are covered with heat-resistant materials.

These materials are designed to withstand thermal shock for only a few seconds until the launch vehicle leaves the launch pad. Once the launch vehicle cleared the launch pedestal, and launch is complete, the entire TPS is replaced and made ready for the next launch.

NASA's launch pad is designed to pump seven truckloads of water per second

The pedestal supporting the launch vehicle can withstand the heat for only a few seconds, but the launch vehicle components have to endure it for several minutes until it reaches orbit. How do they manage to do it?

As the gases escape from the exit of nozzles in launch vehicle, heat is transferred to its surroundings through convection or radiation. The launch vehicle is equipped with navigation systems to monitor its position and adjust the direction of thrust by flexing the nozzle. These components are also covered with TPS layers to shield them from the heat. The protective thermal insulation systems have multiple layers, similar to a workman's glove when lifting hot iron in a blacksmith shop.

Concorde planes traveling at high speeds were not permitted to land at certain airports due to the high vibration during landing. Similarly, does the launch vehicle cause any vibrations? One student shared his experience of traveling abroad.

The launch vehicle generates high thrust which creates vibration and sometimes even shock waves. The surrounding buildings are designed to withstand these vibrations. Additionally, the cameras that capture the launch vehicle footage we see on television are housed in a glass case to protect them from the vibrations and heat of the launch vehicle. This provides us with a clear video of the launch vehicle taking off.

A heat shield that protects the satellite from the atmospheric frictional heat until it crosses the Earth's atmosphere.

I saw that there is a cone-shaped object on the top of the launch vehicle, why this is required?

Normally, when riding a two-wheeler without a helmet, you have to face wind resistance. If a racer participating in a two-wheeler race goes without a helmet, there is a high chance that the wind will tear the muscles in their face above a certain speed.

However, when a launch vehicle tears through the air, its speed increases from 1,000 to 10,000 kilometers per hour as it ascends in altitude. Air friction at this speed generates frictional heat at the top of the shield. Heat shield systems are provided above the payload to protect against that heat.

Additionally, there is a possibility of damage to the satellites and manned spacecraft carried by the launch vehicle due to excessive sound and vibrations during the journey. Therefore, the interior of the pay load fairing is designed to withstand the acoustic loads, much like the air-conditioned coach of a high-speed train that does not hear the noise outside.

A student was on his way to the next place, happy to have the answer to his long-standing doubt about why it is so quiet that we cannot hear anything while traveling in an airtight space like an air-conditioned coach on a train or airplane.

11
Controlling

We explored ways to stack launch vehicles one on top of the other, and then move them from vehicle assembly building to the launch pedestal. Despite our two pairs of eyes, it was incredible to see the huge multi-ton launch vehicle moving along the track like an elephant.

Once the launch vehicle reached the pedestal, we learned about the necessary thermal protection systems required for its continued journey. However, we still had doubts about how it would reach its final destination. The manager indirectly informed the students where they would be going next.

As we waited, a scientist arrived with several toys and announced that someone would explain how the launch vehicle, which had just left the launch site, would be controlled during its journey.

A launch vehicle takes off from a launch pad on Earth and begins its journey through the atmosphere. We learned that as long as there is an atmosphere, there will be air friction.

Despite the wind in the atmosphere, it does not always blow uniformly. One student remarked that sometimes it blows strongly, and other times it sneaks up like a tiger, recalling the proverb "Sow the seed in the Aadi Month for bountiful harvest" and "Make use of wind that blows."

"You are absolutely right." The wind speed can vary up to 70 km above the ground and changes every day and month. When we placed the launch vehicle on the launch pad, it could withstand a certain wind speed. However, a few days before the launch, if strong winds were expected, the launch vehicle would be moved inside the building where it was assembled, instead of remaining on the pedestal.

Balloons are launched daily from morning to evening to predict wind direction and speed. We analyze the data to determine how wind conditions vary over time and whether there are any patterns between past data and the launch date and time. Once the launch vehicle takes off, we guide it on how to shape its trajectory.

A boy innocently asked, "Does the launch vehicle operate on its own with only a given command? Won't you give any advice on where to go during the ascend phase?

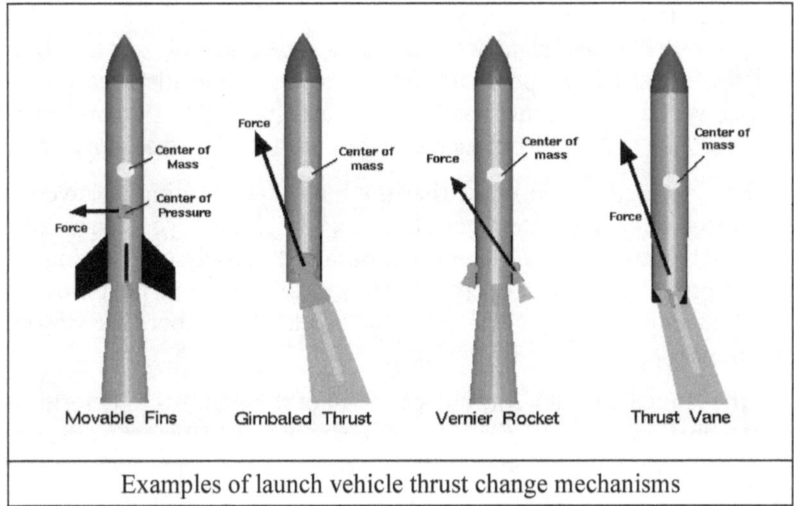

Examples of launch vehicle thrust change mechanisms

As the launch vehicle begins its journey, high air friction can lead to increased energy expenditure. If the vehicle travels in the same direction as the wind, frictional force can be reduced, resulting in lower energy requirements, just like swimming along the flow of river. Conversely, attempting to travel against the wind, similar to swimming upstream, requires a great deal of energy and puts higher aerodynamic loads on the vehicle's structure due to increased air frictional force. This force can cause the structure that support the launch vehicle to break.

Therefore, the launch vehicle's trajectory is designed to maintain a certain angle between the vehicle's path and the wind direction. The launch vehicle is provided with sufficient wind data for several days, including the direction and speed of the wind. Based on this data, the launch vehicle uses the automatic computer installed on it to decide on its path and continue its journey.

"How does this floating launch vehicle determine its path?"

He asked the student. "Bring your friend over here," he continued. "I'll give you a game to play where you both stand in different parts of the arena, and you can only use controls such as right, left, forward, backward, and distance to guide your friend to your location.

Tell your friend to turn right and walk straight for three steps. The student called his friend over, instructing him to turn left and take four steps. These directions are sufficient for navigating on the ground, but if the launch vehicle is in the air and creates a point in space, it can move in any of the three directions.

Take a look at the corner of this arena's wall. Two walls run from the corner to the left and right at the bottom, while one wall runs upwards. All three walls have position sensors to track the distance of the launch vehicle. The launch vehicle calculates its acceleration every few milliseconds to travel from its starting point to the next destination.

For instance, if you know that the bus you are riding is traveling at a speed of 60 kilometers per hour in a straight line, you can predict that it will move one kilometer every minute. Similarly, by knowing the thrust provided by the launch vehicle, you can predict its next move in the next millisecond by calculating its acceleration. There are various methods for predicting acceleration.

The launch vehicle's computer uses all of these inputs to determine its destination. Once that is determined, is the trajectory any different from the pre-planned one programmed into the computer? If there is a difference, the launch vehicle will attempt to steer towards the intended trajectory by deflecting the burnt gases from the engine in the desired direction. The launch vehicle is equipped with various systems to redirect the burnt gases for the required maneuvering.

This room has an automatic air conditioning system set to maintain a temperature of 24 degrees. However, the amount of cold air required to keep the room at 24 degrees varies depending on the number of people present, due to their body heat.

When there are fewer people, the air conditioner runs for a shorter time to keep the room at 24 degrees. When more people are in the room, it becomes warmer, and the air conditioner adjusts to generate more cool air to maintain the temperature at 24 degrees. The system includes sensors that detect the room's temperature. Similarly, these control systems track the launch vehicle's trajectory and guide it to its destination.

Controlling the launch vehicle becomes easier as it ascends through the Earth's atmosphere, as wind resistance decreases with upward movement. Once it enters the vacuum of space, the launch vehicle calculates its trajectory based on the thrust generated by the engine. Since the only opposing force in a vacuum is Earth's gravity, the launch vehicle takes it into consideration and determines its upward trajectory. By designing flight paths that leverage the energy of gravity, itineraries can be crafted to achieve the desired orbital path with minimal energy consumption.

The bus driver controls the bus by turning the front wheel to match the curve of the road, and the train's turns as per the track. During takeoff and landing, the pilot only adjusts the wings.

When a student questioned how the launch vehicle is controlled, despite each vehicle having a control system. He asked the student to bring the rolling chair which was kept on the corner of the arena to demonstrate. He aske the student to sit in the chair. And asked him to move forward and backward and explained this movement is called pitch control.

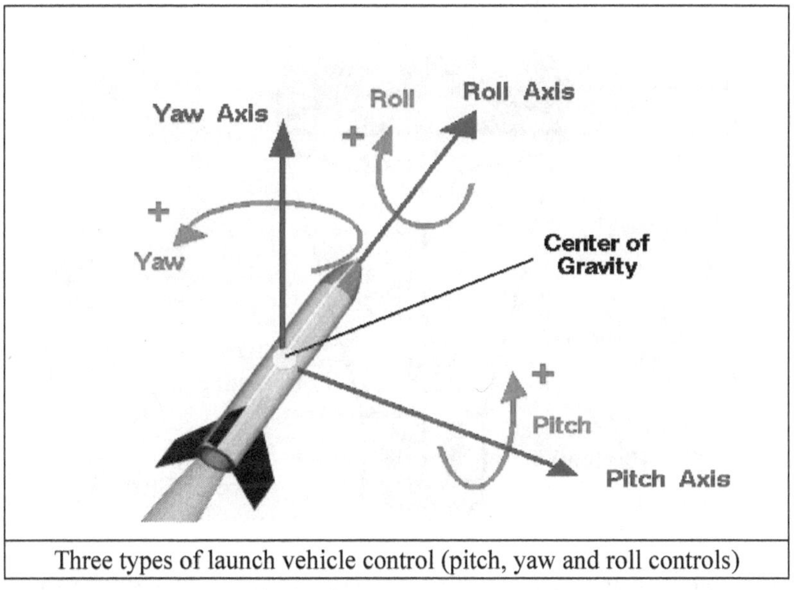

Three types of launch vehicle control (pitch, yaw and roll controls)

Similarly, he asked the student to move sideways and explained the same way yaw control taking place. Finally, the chair was revolved and that was demonstration for roll control. The launch vehicle is controlled using all above three methods.

Does anyone know about the Thanjavur Bobblehead doll? No matter how Thanjavur doll is disturbed from its equilibrium, it would return to its original position. This is what we call stable system. The doll is designed with more mass at the bottom, so all of its weight is transmitted through a specific space at the bottom, which is why Thanjavur doll always end up looking the same.

Similarly, the stability of an object moving through the air depends on the concentration of its weight (center of gravity or CG) and the air pressure (center of pressure or CP) while traveling in the air.

You may have seen a hot air balloon that takes flight using a parachute. The basket for travel and additional heating systems are located at the bottom of the balloon. Because the weight is concentrated downward and the surface area of the balloon is greater at the top, the center of gravity on the balloon is always below center of pressure.

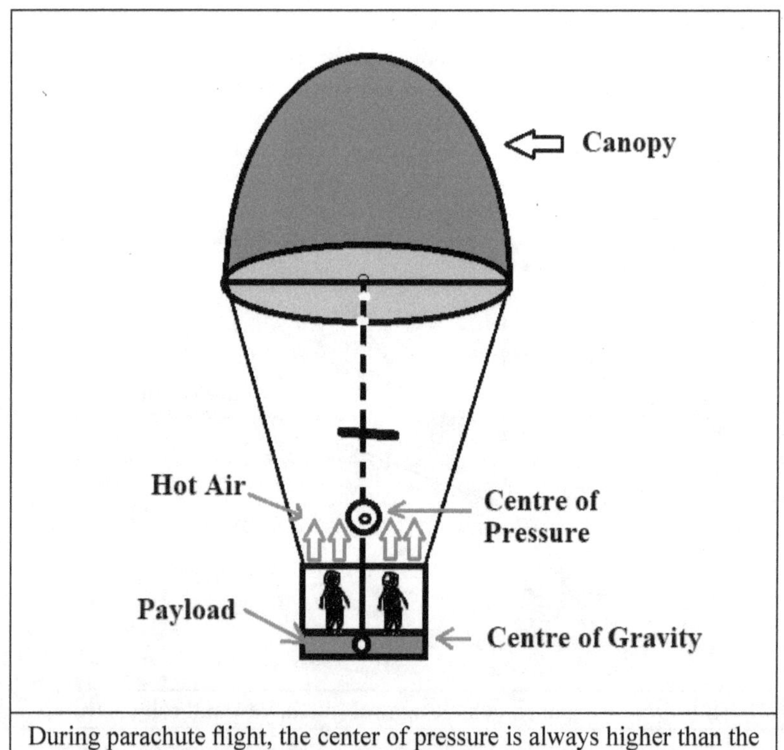

During parachute flight, the center of pressure is always higher than the center of gravity, so it does not overturn.

So no matter how the wind blows and shakes the parachute, the parachute does not fall upside down. Carried by wind blowing from one direction to another.

To control the launch vehicle, it should be unstable system. Hence, at any given time of launch vehicle journey the center of pressure always kept below the center of gravity.

To ensure that, the surface area exposed to the launch vehicle components must be increased. To increase such surface area, the lower part of the launch vehicle is provided with wing designs. Which ensures unstable system and guidance mechanism maneuver the launch vehicle to the required direction.

Can you keep a football to stand in your index finger ? asked the scientist.

A student who is the football player pointed out that I've done this many times between football matches and pointed it out on his index finger.

Can you do it without rolling? It is not possible if it is not rolling. Because the rotation creates a stability, we can hold the rotating object at our fingertips without it falling down. The Earth rotates itself and orbit around the Sun. A similar stabilization system is created for sounding rockets you saw in previous classes. During its journey it revolves it own axis at specified revolution per minute. It is to be noted that in these rockets there are no designs to redirect the burnt gases from the nozzle.

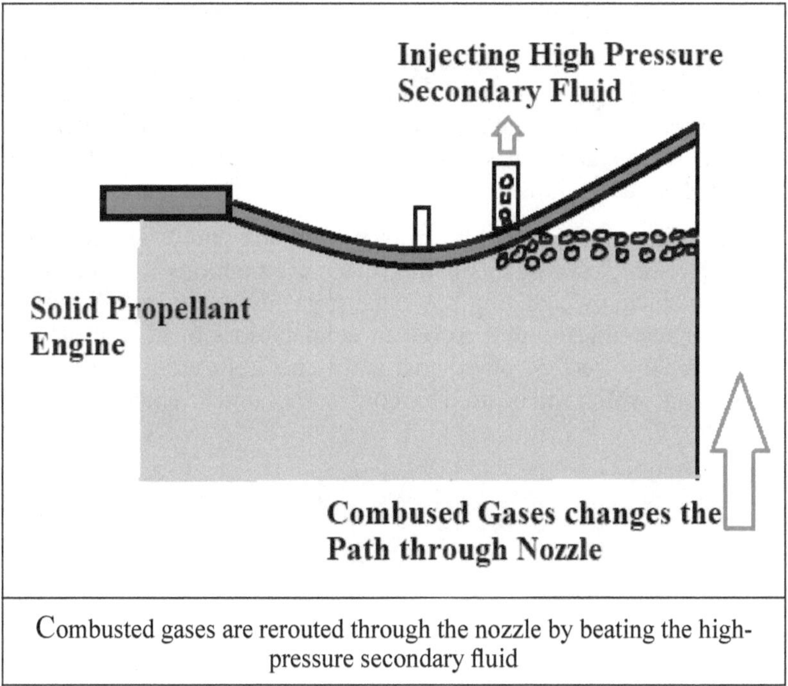

Combusted gases are rerouted through the nozzle by beating the high-pressure secondary fluid

If we place the point of balance of the stick's weight such that it falls on our finger, we can balance the stick. The weight of the stick flows through our finger, keeping it in place. However, if the stick tilts slightly and the point of balance shifts out of our hand, it will fall down.

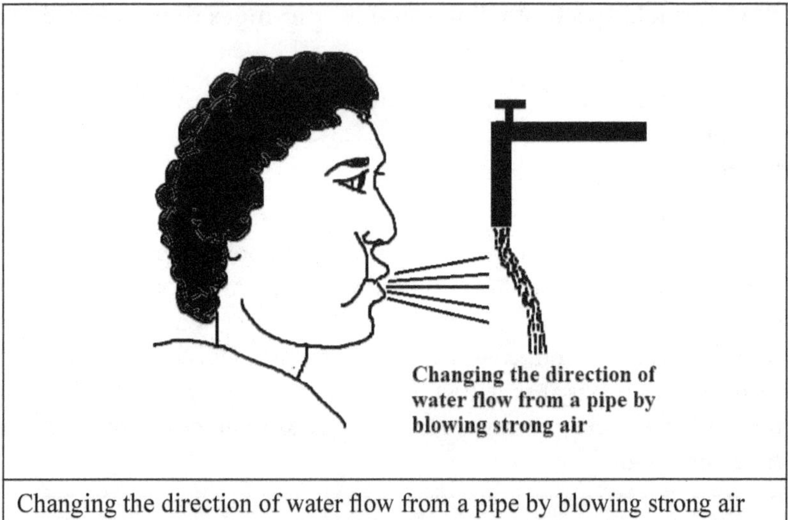

Changing the direction of water flow from a pipe by blowing strong air

Wow! If we think, only the burnt gases used to generate thrust, could such a large launch vehicle be redirected? It's amazing when you think about it. For instance, can I change the direction of water flow here? Once, a student was blowing water from a hose he had used to wash his hands for lunch.

The scientist observed him from behind and said, "You did it very well." He went on to explain that there are methods to control the launch vehicle by changing the exhaust gas direction by using high-pressure secondary liquid stored in solid motors to hit the exhaust gases. When direction of exhaust gases changes the resulting thrust also change which will be used for control the launch vehicle trajectory.

12
What is the cost of a launch vehicle?

They are saying that, given the size of the machines, these launch vehicles will cost crores, won't they? Can our lifetime earnings afford a launch vehicle? Two students were discussing this doubt.

Another student also shared information from a newspaper that today's price of the launch vehicle that took man to the moon may be ten thousand crores. A group of students were preparing to ask the next person why the price was so high.

Since you know a lot about the launch vehicle, today's afternoon session can be used to clear your doubts, and their manager has created a perfect moment for them. A panel of 10 experts welcomed the students to answer their questions.

In previous classes, it was understood that since the launch vehicle carries its own oxygen, the amount of mass it carries to orbit is only one to four percent of its own weight. However, a student interrupted her question by saying that she did not understand why single-use expendable launch vehicles cost more than multi-use or reusable launch vehicle.

"Awesome. But how did you come to the conclusion that the launch vehicle was only used once?" a scientist asked her. "The launch vehicle that took man to the moon did not return!" She also dropped the gist of her question by saying that she had read that they made new launch vehicles every time and that it cost one and a half times the cost of building the Eiffel Tower in France.

"Well, before we get into this, let's go over a few things first," said one of the experts. "A launch vehicle does not only carry satellites and spacecraft to a certain altitude. At that height, it also gives it the kinetic energy it needs to orbit without falling down.

Energy is required when an object is moved to a certain height from the ground. Similarly, to set an object in motion, kinetic energy is given according to the speed at which it is traveling.

An object placed in a circular orbit at a certain height above the earth requires potential energy to get there and kinetic energy to keep it orbiting at a certain speed without falling down. This energy is many times more than what we use in ground transportation. That is why a huge energy requirement is created to keep the space craft in a certain orbit.

Circular Route (km)	Kinetic Energy (MJ/Kg)	Potential Energy (MJ/Kg)	Total Energy Requirement (MJ/Kg)
500	29.87	4.65	33.65
200x36000	52.45	2	54.45
36000	4.70	53.2	57.9

The energy required to propel it into space. Since parts of the launch vehicle travel from half the distance to full, the launch vehicle will require anywhere from 30 to 100 times more energy than this.

At the time of the invention of the launch vehicle, there were expendable vehicles. For the first time in the 1980s, NASA (National Aeronautics and Space Administration) developed a reusable space shuttle. The solid motors of the launch vehicle were also recovered from the sea, but due to reliability issues, they were not reused.

It is noteworthy that the space shuttle was only 6 percent of the total weight of the launch vehicle. After that, all other launch vehicle parts are generally not returned. Depending on the design of the launch vehicle, the cost of manufacturing the components and the fuel required varies.

Even in solid motor, the nozzles and motor are highly damaged during action, so reusing them is not beneficial. In contrast, liquid-fueled engines can be brought back and refurbished in a matter of days for reuse on the launch vehicle.

Similarly, when stages of launch vehicle separated beyond the Earth's atmosphere, they are more likely to burn up due to excessive air friction when entering to the atmosphere. However, safely bringing back the ground lift liquid engine stages which separated at Earth's atmosphere region has been successful.

Therefore, we can bring back liquid fuel engines because of their advantages over solid motor.

In liquid engines, we can inject fuel according to our need and reduce the thrust, similar to changing the amount of petrol according to the speed of a car when traveling. Consequently, in a launch vehicle, the detached primary stage can be brought back slowly towards the Earth.

As it approaches Earth, the separated stage can reduce its propulsive power by burning less of the liquid fuel in its engines. When the engines are operated to produce only the thrust equal to the weight of the burnout stage, the separated stage trajectory is adjusted so that it slows down instead of plummeting toward Earth. However, not all fluid engines are designed to throttle required level. It is worth noting that less than 10 percent of the liquid engine in the world today have such a variable thrust design.

In the case of a launch vehicle with multiple engines, the process can be simplified. It can be compared to a pitcher pumping water into a well. If the force exerted on the rope is greater than the weight of the water in the pitcher, the pitcher will rise to the top. Conversely, if the force is less, the pitcher will go down. By applying the force equivalent to the weight of the pitcher, the water pitcher stays in one place without moving up and down.

Bringing the burnt-out falcon launch vehicle first stage safely without falling by operating its liquid engines partially.

The first stage of the launch vehicle is re-engineered for reusability and re-used multiple times. In this way, SpaceX, America's private space company, has successfully reduced the cost of launch vehicle by more than 40 percent.

You mentioned that the space shuttle was also reused in a similar way, so why is it not in use anymore?

When the space shuttle was first built, the program was created with the assumption that increased use would reduce the cost of going into space. However, the project was eventually abandoned due to unforeseen accidents and the fact that bringing the space shuttle back to Earth did not actually reduce material costs.

Seventy percent of the cost of a vehicle is attributed to its first stage of any vehicle. Therefore, SpaceX has demonstrated that its reusable method can cut the cost of the vehicle in half by safely landing and reusing it. Additionally, efforts are being made to reduce the cost of the vehicle by returning the heat shield used to protect the materials carried in the launch vehicle."

Falcon heavy launch vehicle stage built with number of small liquid engines to obtain high thrust.

"Is there any difference between designing components for a launch vehicle and designing things we use at home, especially due to the high cost?" a student asked.

When designing any material, it is typically designed to withstand several times more than its intended use, taking into account factors such as load capacity. For example, the weight limit of a bicycle wheel is usually indicated on it. A bicycle is designed to carry one or two people, not five, and even heavier people typically weigh less than 150 kg, so its two wheels are made to support up to 200 kg.

Overloading a car with too much stuff can cause its suspension to fail, just as lifting too much weight can cause back pain problems. When designing a car, the weight of the car, the weight of the passengers, and the weight of the cargo are all taken into account, and the car frame is designed to bear 50-100% more weight.

The more factors that are taken into account, the heavier the material needs to be. Therefore, to reduce unnecessary weight in the design of a launch vehicle, its parts are typically designed to withstand only 20-25% more weight than what needs to be carried and the forces generated by wind. .

Another expensive part of the launch vehicle is the pay load fairing which is safely brough back.

"You have all traveled by train many times. How do you sleep in the middle berth in a sleeping compartment?" the scientist asked.

"I've noticed that if we get a middle berth, we always have a chain to hold it in place before going to sleep. Has anyone ever noticed chain being cut and middle berth falling down while you were sleeping? " the speaker asked.

After much discussion, they replied that they had not heard of anyone cutting the chain. A chain designed to support a 100-kg human would remain stable even if an elephant lay down on it. The price paid for this stability is the weight and cost of making the chain.

The components of a launch vehicle are unlike anything else and are made of lightweight and high-strength materials. Iron has a density of 7.8 g/cc, while aluminum has a density of 2.7 g/cc, which can create a lightweight material that can perform the same job as iron. Composite materials with densities below 2.0 g/cc are leading the way in making launch vehicle structures. These materials are also widely used in airplanes.

"Are all launch vehicles designed the same way?" someone asked.

"No. man rated launch vehicles are designed to be safer than cargo launch vehicles, so their components are slightly stronger. They also have many ways to escape crew in case of danger," the scientist replied.

"Is each part of the launch vehicle individually tested, and are all stages tested on Earth to their full potential before being allowed to carry humans?" someone asked.

"Yes. The launch vehicle is tested for reliability before carrying humans. Each part is individually tested, and each stage is checked several times on Earth to ensure its full potential. If any flaws are found during these tests, they are rectified before the launch vehicle is used for human transport," the speaker explained.

After discussing launch vehicles, someone asked about the general differences between a launch vehicle and a missile. The speaker suggested taking a break for tea and continuing the discussion in the next class.

13

The Missile and the Launch Vehicle

As you had learned in the first training class, rocket technology is named according to the application for which it is used. There are many types of missiles, and the first type of missile determines its landing location upon launch.

To illustrate this, the instructor called a student to throw a stone. The stone was thrown at an oblique angle, rising high and then falling back down from the height it had reached, landing far away from the throwing location. The first type of missile is launched in a similar manner to how the student threw the stone."

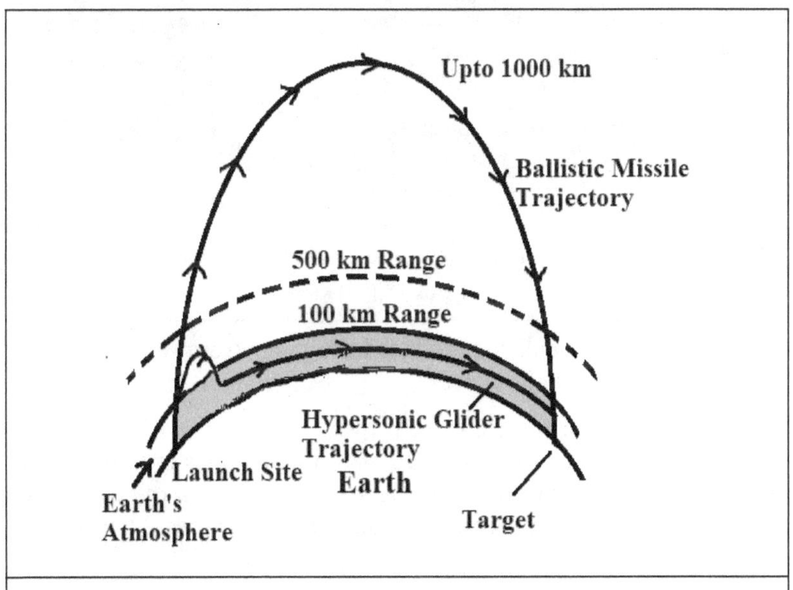

It is concluded that need an aircraft engine to match the trajectory of the missile ? Or do you need a rocket engine ?

There are three stages involved in missile deployment. The first stage is the rocket engine, which propels the payload into the sky at high speed. This first step typically takes two to five minutes, and a higher thrust force will quickly lift the missile out of the atmosphere.

In the second stage, the missile continues its journey until it reaches above the atmosphere. The travel time for this stage varies from five minutes to half an hour, depending on the distance the missile has to travel.

In the last stage, the weapons designed to hit the enemy are separated from the missile and released at a specific angle. Usually, No thrust is imparted to them, and they rely on the Earth's gravity to move from a certain height towards the surface, hitting the target with force. Missiles of this type do not require precision strikes, as they are equipped with nuclear payload capable of causing high damage. They are capable of causing damage several kilometers around a target if they fall on it.

RS-28 is the world's longest- range intercontinental ballistic missile with a range of 18,000 kms.

Intercontinental ballistic missiles have range from several hundred kilometers to 15,000 kilometers.

The next type of missile travels through the atmosphere and does not require rocket engines. Instead, turbo jet engines are used, which propel the missile forward using the oxygen present in the air. As they travel through the air, they move at a slightly slower speed than a rocket powered missiles.

However, these types of missiles are capable of changing their destination as per the need. They have a tendency to maneuver and attack, just like the way an airplane bends when command is given to chase and destroy a target.

Not only this, missiles are also classified according to their speed of travel, with some being subsonic and others slightly faster than the speed of sound. Missiles are categorized into various types, ranging from one to three times the speed of sound to more than five times the speed of sound. Some missiles can travel at a speed of 10,000 kilometers per hour if they need to attack at the time of war.

Similarly, there are missiles that are structured and designed to evade detection from all available detection methods of the enemy. Missiles are designed for surface-to-surface (Agni series missiles), ground-to-sky (Akash and Trishul), and sky-to-sky (Astra) purposes, and can be launched from anywhere, including the air, water, or land.

When a missile is headed towards a country, there are missiles equipped with technology to destroy it mid-flight, rather than allowing it to enter the country. Such missiles possess more precise control systems than launch vehicles.

A student was expressing her understanding to her friends about how profound Einstein's statement was regarding the prediction of efficient missiles in every country during that period itself, as she had read an article in newspaper many years before in which reporter had once asked Einstein about what kind of weapons would be used in World War III. He had replied, "I don't know what weapons will be there in World War III, but surely there will be stone and mud in the fourth world war."

14
Farewell

The Examination was conducted at the end of the training, and all the student answered the questions well and passed.

One boy vowed to build a rover that could travel to Mars in future. Similarly, another girl envisioned setting up a transportation company that could travel faster than airplanes and transport vehicles from one part of the world to another in just half an hour.

Another student was racking his brain as to why this field has not progressed since learning that the launch vehicle that carried man into space sixty years ago and the speed of the launch vehicle that traveled to Mars this year was 40 thousand kilometers per hour. Like other fields, he hopes to develop a high-speed launch vehicle in the future and reach the next galaxy as close to us as the Sun to see if anyone is surviving there.

Yet another boy was eager to create a tourism industry that would enable middle-class people to build low-cost launch vehicles and travel into space, so that ordinary people can fly on an airplane at least once.

Thus, for everyone, these training classes initiated a new beginning in their lives.

Appreciating the enthusiasm and discipline of the students who attended the training, the manager awarded certificates to all of them.